FOR VOICE
(The Beach, Fall, Re-cite,
The Ant-Killers)

Severo Sarduy

Latin American Literary Review Press
Yvette E. Miller
Editor

FOR VOICE
(The Beach, Fall, Re-cite, The Ant-Killers)

Severo Sarduy

Translated by Philip Barnard

LATIN AMERICAN LITERARY REVIEW PRESS
SERIES: DISCOVERIES
PITTSBURGH, PENNSYLVANIA 1985

The Latin American Literary Review Press publishes Latin American creative writing under the series title *Discoveries*, and critical works under the series title *Explorations*.

Originally published as *Para la voz,* Editorial Fundamentos, 1978.

Library of Congress Cataloging in Publication Data

Sarduy, Severo.
    For voice.

    Translation of: Para la voz.
    Contents: The beach — Fall — Recite — [etc.]
    I. Title.
PQ7390.S28P313   1984   862   84-26137
ISBN   0-935480-20-X

This project is supported by a grant from the National Endowment for the Arts in Washington, D.C., a federal agency.

CONTENTS

Translator's Preface 9

Chronology 12

The Beach 13

Fall 57

Re-cite 85

The Ant-Killers 111

TRANSLATOR'S PREFACE

For Voice is a modest example of the work of a writer not nearly so well known in the United States as he ought to be, despite the growing popularity, and popularization, over the past few years, of the Latin American novel. The very modernity — a term as misleading as it is useful — of Severo Sarduy's writing is no doubt an important factor in this relative lack of exposure, although readers in Latin America and Europe have long been more familiar with him than has the North American audience.[1] This «modernity» has fostered a curious, two-sided relationship between Sarduy's writing, a still-growing corpus of novels, essays, drama, and poetry, and its audience. On the one hand, Sarduy's most salient qualities have placed him in the vanguard of contemporary Hispanic literature. His novels are notable for their remarkable, direct foregrounding of the linguistic, hence rhetorical and artificial, nature of the literary act, their highly informed continuation of the baroque, Gongoran tradition in Spanish-language literature, and their effective conjugation of certain formal aspects of contemporary European writing with that tradition. These novels are examples of a writing whose modernity is not a disembodied and abstract verbalism, but on the contrary an energetic, sexuated, corporal approach to literary experience. *From Cuba With a Song* and *Cobra*, for example, are rightly considered to be classics in their genre. In an English-language context, Melville, or to an even greater degree Laurence Sterne, with his amalgam of serio-comic lucidity and formal expertise, might offer parallels to these digressive but highly structured and engaging texts.

At the same time, the qualities that have established these works' reputations have also separated Sarduy from the mainstream of Latin American literature, particularly insofar as it is defined, for the North American audience, vis-a-vis a particular social and historical situation onto which the nineteenth- and twentieth-century tradition of novelistic realism, socialist or otherwise, still casts a long shadow. Sarduy's writing intrigues, pleases, or displeases us *as* literature, rather than entertaining a sort of generalized *regionalism* that would entertain us with its exoticism, or with the historical fiction of a regional or national experience coming to know itself, growing and gaining self-consciousness both as literature and as community. To describe

Sarduy's situation in terms of American literature, this attitude is akin to the notion that Faulkner is not so much a writer as a spiritual historian of «the South,» an aesthetic witness to some grave and elevating inner evolution or decadence.

Sarduy's Caribbean provenance, in other words, has an essential but non-ideological impact on his writing (one could say that his writing is destructive of ideologies), which is what Roland Barthes pointed out when he noted that Sarduy's writing is not from Cuba, but from the Cuban language. It is well known that Sarduy is systematically ignored by official anthologies of Cuban literature, for whom he seems to have become a «Frenchman» (!). But this should hardly be surprising in the case of a writer whose work exemplifies a displacement of literature onto a negative, plural, empty movement of language, rather than repressing that movement, suppressing literature (in other words rhetoric) in favor of its ostensible aesthetic or ideological value. Sarduy's affirmation of a certain pleasure in writing, and his recognition of the libidinal investments that the institution of literature more often masks than manifests, are far from the didacticism of ethico-moral and hermeneutic conceptions of the literary text, whether those conceptions are produced in the context of a Marxist nostalgia for order, or in the academic and aestheticizing bias of the Anglo-American discourse on literature. Sarduy's situation, to cite Barthes once again, is clear, for he «merits all of the adjectives that make up the lexicon of literary quality. His texts are bright, lively [allègre], sensitive, humorous, inventive, innovative, and nonetheless clear, even cultural, continuously affectionate. Yet I fear that if it were a question of being received without difficulties in well-bred literary society, he would lack that necessary suspicion of remorse, that nothing of a fault, that shadow of a signified, that transforms writing into a lesson and recuperates it as 'fine art'....»

As radio-plays, written between the mid-1960's and the mid-1970's, the four texts in *For Voice* are an attempt to adapt the concerns of contemporary literature to the genre of radio-drama, and it is fair to say that few such attempts have been as successful as Sarduy's. Besides Beckett's contributions to the genre, such as *All That Fall, Words and Music,* or *Cascando,* it is difficult to cite other examples of the same caliber. *The Beach, Fall, Re-cite,* and *The Ant-Killers* have been produced in Spanish, French, German, and English (by the BBC, in translations by Barbara Thompson); they have received several of the most prestigious awards granted for radio-drama in Europe, notably the Prix Italia (in 1975, for *Re-cite,* in a production by Radio France's Atelier de Création Radiophonique); and, in the case of *The Beach,* have been adapted for the stage. In a country where the most unknown and impoverished of the muses is that of radio-drama, a production of these plays would be a long-overdue and welcome event. And in any case, *For Voice* invites speculation on the meagre attention received by this genre — which of course depends essentially on the written and spoken word — in the United States, which is to say in a community whose aversion to self-consciously rhetorical modes of discourse is fundamental, and whose investment in the image as a reproduction of the real, in the form of television and cinema, is so massive as to constitute a cultural phenomenon.

Philip Barnard

1. Two of Sarduy's novels have appeared in English, in excellent translations by Suzanne Jill Levine: *De donde son los cantantes,* published as *From Cuba with a Song* (in *Triple Cross*; E.P. Dutton, 1973); and *Cobra* (E.P. Dutton, 1975).

Chronology

1936: Severo Sarduy born in Camagüey, Cuba.

1950-60: Publishes poetry and, after the Revolution, in 1959-60, becomes a contributor to *Lunes de Revolución*, a literary weekly directed by Guillermo Cabrera Infante.

1960: Arrives in France to study at the Ecole du Louvre.

1963: *Gestos*, a novel.

1964-67: Completes his studies with a thesis on Flavian art and establishes himself in Paris. Becomes a member of two important literary groups centered around the reviews *Mundo Nuevo*, directed by Emir Rodríguez Monegal, and *Tel Quel*, the most influential French literary journal of the sixties and seventies.

1967: *De donde son los cantantes (From Cuba With a Song)*, a novel.

1969: *Escrito sobre un cuerpo,* essays; *Flamenco,* poems.

1970: *Mood Indigo,* poems.

1971: *Les Merveilles de la Nature,* poems, with drawings by Leonor Fini. Awarded the Prix Paul Gilson for *La Playa (The Beach)*, a radio-play.

1972: *Cobra*, a novel, awarded the Prix Medici étranger in a French translation by Philippe Sollers and the author. Awarded the Prix Italia for *Relato (Re-cite)*, a radio-play. *La Playa* is produced in a German stage version, directed by Deryk Mendel.

1973: *L'Epingleuse,* poems.

1974: *Big Bang,* poems.

1975: *Barroco,* essays.

1977: *La Playa* is produced in a French stage version, directed by Simone Benmussa with the Compagnie Renaud-Barrault.

1978: *Para la voz (For Voice)*, radio-plays.

1980: *Maitreya,* a novel.

1981: *La doublure,* essays; *Tanka,* a radio-play.

1984: *Colibri,* a novel.

THE BEACH

Speeches placed beneath one another and italicized are to be spoken simultaneously. Although extra brackets are occasionally used to indicate this effect, the delivery should be the same throughout the text, even when the italicized phrases are not identical. The desired effect is one of rhythmic counterpoint, the «intelligibility» of the phrase being secondary in these cases. — Tr.

The Beach is a succession of sequences, or of transformations of a single sequence, which, by means of those variations, becomes changed into its opposite. None of these sequences, then, can be considered «primary» or «true»; none are «original.» The sole reality is the constant transformation of the narrative, its development, its continual metamorphosis.

The play's title *[La Playa]* refers to the spaces which separate the recorded areas on a phonograph record; bands of silence, symbolic «blanks» or white spaces *[blancos]* in a black circle.

In each band or «beach» *[playa]* the sequence is restructured and one of its details varied or transformed into its opposite. In each band the narrative begins from zero; it erases, retracts, and denies what has been written previously, and imposes a new version. There is no final outcome, for the different versions have equivalent values. Like a figure on the page being effaced by another inscription, the final result should be the annullment of the sequence itself, its disappearance in a cycle of versions that succeed and contradict one another.

There are no characters, properly speaking, for psychology and dramatic coherence are, like the rest of the play's events and setting, entirely at the mercy of the transformations. Rather, the characters are treated as actants, as bearers of texts.

There are six of these actants, although this figure is, in a sense, debatable:

Man 1 and Man 2 are the same actant in different periods. Man 2 is the present (his discourse unfolds in this tense); Man 1 is the future, he speaks from and beginning with the future, and thus his discourse unfolds in the past, in the form of uncertain, wavering memories. The same situation occurs with Women 1 and 2. Man 3 and Woman 3 speak indiscriminately in the present or the past.

If the first four actants (M1 and M2, W1 and W2) tend to coalesce, the two remaining actants (M3 and W3) tend to double themselves. Man 3, who in the first sequences shows off his youth and gigolo's body, changes into a mature admirer and customer of such bodies; Woman 3, who is the first sequences is the mature admirer, subsequently becomes the young woman who..., and so on. Both actants, in short, change their functions.

These variations on a theme imply a musical structure. Hence the melodic organization of the sequences and the superposition of voices and of sentences on the page.

The Beach is also a hommage to the naked body and to the beachside panoply. I have attempted to shape this universe with a minimum of elements, with a reduced, repetitive, «empty» vocabulary. The baroque is the natural tendency of Spanish. To empty out the sentence is, once again, to postulate literature as artifice.

M1. blue,

M2. green,

W1. yellow,

W2. brown,

M3. white,

W3. red,

M2. umbrellas all along the beach, still fringes, circles, canvas on the moving fringe of the water. Water, white fringe, moving on the sand, advancing, receding, still for an instant, and then back under the row of circles; the water, slack, striped by the fringe of the smacks, wake of foam whiter than the sand, fading, written on the canvas, still, caught by the Instamatic, *do you remember?*

M1. *do you remember?* I was walking, we were walking, we were running on the sand, the most conventional picture of love, race on the sand, color film, holiday photos, faded gestures, fading, caught by the Instamatic, publicity picture, your hair down, picture of happiness, blue on the blue of the water, green on the green of the water, and above, in black letters, straight, AMBRE, in a white rectangle, then in another white rectangle, underneath, SOLAIRE.

We were laughing.

M2. *We were laughing.*

M1. You ran ahead, I caught up with you, we were laughing, I caught up with you, there, I was laughing, *I caught up with you*

M2. *I caught up with you,* here, now, your hair, the sound of the water, caught, faded, us, by the Instamatic, picture of happiness, AMBRE SOLAIRE, *I remember.*

W2.   *I remember.*

W1.   *I remember.*

M3.   I remember. I was sleeping.

W1.   On the sand, the moving fringe of the water, caught by the Instamatic, wet your feet; we were running, *we were headed toward each other.*

M3.   *we were headed toward each other.*

M1.   each

W3.   toward

W1.   the other

M1.   *each*

M3.   *each*

W1.   *toward*

M3.   *toward*

W2.   *the other*

M3.   *the other*

SEQUENCE II

W1.   you were on the sand,

M3.   you were coming closer.

W1.   *I was walking,*

M3.   *you were walking.*

W1.   In the white light, colors were evaporating, shapes were dissolving,

18

everything was decomposing, wasting away: overexposed photo, edges eaten away, white on white. The sky stretched taut; the streaks of rattling single-prop planes: behind, floating, the texts, on streamers, attached to the tail, rippling: the enormous letters, black, HAPPY HOLIDAYS WITH THE EXPRESS,

W2.   HAPPY
HOLIDAYS WITH THE EXPRESS.

M1. STUYVESANT, SO MUCH FRESHER.

M2. STUYVESANT, SO MUCH FRESHER.

M1. *You appeared.*

W1. *You appeared.*

M3. I was sleeping on the sand, drunk perhaps. What time is it?, I asked. The tide was rising, trailing rocks, bottles, dead fish, oranges. You could hear laughter, the noise of an airplane engine. I was sleeping. Drunk perhaps.

M1. *Drunk perhaps.*

W1. *Drunk perhaps.*

M3. *Drunk perhaps.*

M3. A couple of tourists. They were watching me. My most professional smile. I asked the time. The tide was rising. My feet among the rocks, the oranges, the dead fish.

M1. At present, I recall very precisely; too much so. A sharp, blinding, millemetric picture, of drugs. A written picture. I remember. The sky was *Bazile blue, Gigou blue, Dufy blue.*

M2.   *Bazile blue, Gigou blue, Dufy blue.*

M2. We're heading toward you. You're sleeping on the sand. Its very early. The Arab is setting up the black metal tables in the sand, the orange-striped umbrellas. A brown waiter goes by, a flowered napkin in his belt; the jukebox starts spouting Brazilian music; the water is rising;

we're speaking Italian; trailing seashells, rocks, hunks of rotten wood.

W2. Non-oily tanning lotion, allows ultra-rapid tanning of normal or oily skin, protects against sunburn. Tones up the skin without oilness. Instant relief from sunburn pain. Apply frequently before and during exposure to the sun. 60 degrees.

M1. The tide was rising.

W1. A bird went by.

M1. *He was lying on the sand, naked.*

W1. *He was lying on the sand, naked.*

W1. *Naked.*

W2. *Naked.*

M1. *Blond.*

M2. *Blond.*

M1. *On the sand.*

W1. *On the sand.*

M2. *On the sand.*

W2. *On the sand.*

SEQUENCE III

W1. *Sound and Light of France. The Riviera, miracle of*

W2. *Sound and Light of France. The Riviera, miracle of nature. Cannes (Maritime Alps). The beach at dawn.*

W1. We were walking. He was sleeping.

M1. The flow of things.

M2. The ebb of images. Visible things, diurnal, and their double that returns, empty, in sleep. Slow images, blurred copies: your body inverted in sleep, shifting, unfaithful.

M1. The flow of voices.

M2. The ebb of the echo. The voice, volume, vase, copper circle. Its deaf reflection, metallic shadow in sleep. The space of the voice, blind.

M1. *The flow of glances. The flow of gestures.*

M2. *The flow of glances. The flow of gestures.*

M1. We were walking. *Picture postcard.* The bay was an empty

M2.   *Picture postcard.*
theatre. He was sleeping. The sound of a passing plane, or of the jukebox, or of a car, far away, with that of the rising tide, repeated, woke him. He jumped up. All three of us laughed.

W1. The Arab was setting up the umbrellas. I looked at you. Another time.

W2. *The ebb of gestures.* The black metal tables. Carving

W1. *The ebb of gestures.*   zones of shadow
with the orange and white-striped canvases, obscure diamonds on the sand, circles in the reverberation. He brought glasses filled with fruit, cakes, water, cool drinks.

W2. A child goes by, carrying a pile of white rubber. He blows it up patiently. It's a boat. Another fills his pail in the rising wave, empties it in the sand a little farther on, and fills it again. He speaks to us in German. He asks us the time. *The ebb of gestures.*

W1.   *The ebb of gestures.*

M2. Why continue the conversation? *Picture postcard.*

M1.   *Picture postcard.*

M2. *So much fresher.*

W1. *Before and during exposure to the sun.*

M2. *With the Express.*

W2. *At dawn.*

M3. What time is it?, I asked.

W1. He was drunk.

M2. And then came the souvenir photo.

M3. Its an Instamatic.

W1. He remarked.

M3. Another one.

W1. He says.

M3. Smile, I said.

M1. And then the race on the sand. The most conventional picture of happiness. The publicity photo.

W1. He followed us. I remember. That night, we met again at the bar. *The ebb of gestures.*

W2. *The ebb of gestures.*

W2. The broken glass.

M2. The silence. One second.

W2. *The blood.*

M2. *The blood.*

SEQUENCE IV

M1. *I remember.*

W1. *I remember.*

W2. Look. Look. Blood.

M1. The cut on his foot, the splinters of glass, the red stain on the mat, fresh. I rushed over to him.

W2. The salty mouth, buzzing in your ears, worse on the inside. The color draining away.

M1. You fell. He was laughing, bleeding. He'd crossed his legs. Someone was picking the pieces of glass out of the sole of his foot. He had a cognac. The tape. The music again. You came to. Another cognac. We laughed. Someone was picking the pieces of glass out, with love, with care. Sharp red lines across his foot, spreading over the skin. Over the sole of his foot, a trickle, flowing red, bright, thick. He was laughing.

W1. Then, the foot bandaged, he fell on the sand, in silence. He fell asleep. I was watching him. *A child went by with a bird.*

W2.   *A child went by with a bird.*
     The tide was rising.

M1. *We walked along the shore.*

W1. *We walked along the shore.* Collecting green-black stones, rust-colored, pieces of glass polished by the sea. We wanted to find a Flavian coin, a stone with an engraved name, a fragment of an Ionian face, an acanthus leaf, an ivory tablet.

M1. A Byzantine marble, with red and white veins, symmetrical, showing a fish, a pair of eyes, in concentric circles, still, warching me, *or my own face.*

W1.   *or my own*
     face.

23

M1. But every find was a farce, the parody of the searched-for object, a derisive equivalent of desire, its counterfeit image, atrophied, ridiculous. We were laughing.

W1. *We found,*

M1. *We found,* in the stagnant water of the reefs — greenish circles, scummy foam, in decomposition — on the trembling edge of the pools, stinking food tins; beer bottles with bloated labels, whitish, washed out, like diseased skin; crushed bottlecaps; Kodak wrappers; ameboid plastic bottles, orange, shining, almost phosphorescent, like dead fish, with curling handles, alive, with serpent-headed lids: Orange bottles, with faded inscriptions, eaten away by the salt, until only a few silvery lumps remain; white islands that were part of a letter, sometimes no more than a period, a clear halo on the yellow background, a printed stripe, nothing.

W1. The tide was rising, dragging this debris, these scraps, these leavings of the palpable, parodies *of our searches.*

M1.   *of our searches.* We had returned our finds to the sea, throwing the stones and the pieces of rotten wood one after the other. *We were laughing.*

W1.   *We were laughing.*
We were running along the beach; jumping over the trash; on the sand, sprinkling ourselves; hugging the reefs, the pools of water, the white bakelite pedalboats that were on the beach, their sharp propellers, aluminum trefoils. We were laughing.

W1. An advertising plane went by.

W2. *So much fresher.*

M2. *So much fresher.*

W1. A child was running, crying something drowned out by *the engine of the plane.*

M1. *the sound of the waves.*

M3. I woke up with a start. Heat. The bandaged foot, white, wet. I remembered. A dream scene: I was running through the night, between black trees. I was suffocating. As I passed by, lizards' white scales, wild beasts' eyes, pallid crescent stripes of fur, glowed fleetingly. They chased me in confusion, to kill me. They were armed with arrows. A spreading smell of poison, mixed with warm sap, and animals; a murmur of voices mixed with humid earth, footsteps muffled by the moss. The birds fleeing. I was afraid. I was crying. I invoked several diurnal deities. I promised. I was sinking into a mire. Suddenly I felt a pain in my foot: an arrow had just pierced it. I woke up, my foot soaked. I was thirsty. I was sweating. The tide was rising. It was early. A couple of tourists were approaching.

W2. What time is it?

M3. She asked me. What time is it? I asked at the same time.
We laughed.

W2. *We laughed.*

SEQUENCE V

W1. A German gigolo.

W2. A latinlover tedesco.

W3. A john.

W1. *Gunther?*

W2. *Gunther?*

W2. *Werner?*

W3. *Werner?*

W3. *Rudolph?*

W1. *Rudolph?*

W1. *From Breme?*

W3. *From Breme?*

W3. *From Dusseldorf?*

W2. *From Dusseldorf?*

W2. *From Berlin?*

W1. *From Berlin?*

W3. There are fewer lamps in my London flat than in my Paris flat, which has fewer balconies facing Fifth Avenue than my New York flat. In the fall I light the lamps in Paris, in winter I shut my balconies in London, New York is insufferable in summer.

M3. And Casablanca?

W3. Not bad.

M3. And Marakesh?

W3. Nice.

M3. And Cairo?

W3. Its alright.

M3. And Istanbul?

W3. They have gold chamberpots there. Of solid gold, in the old harem. They had hundreds of houris, eunuchs, and all sorts of little darlings. At Hagia Sophia there's a cold window. They eat yogurt with everything.

M3. Me, with some dollars, I'd take a trip around the world. New York. Hawaii. Rio. I can't take any more winters in Hamburg and summers in Cannes. With some dollars, we could go dancing tonight. But you see, I'm still waiting. Yep, they owe me, and not just for a stand-in either. For «Opium and Flagellation in the Dock Districts», my latest film, in color; but the check hasn't come, and I've even got to find someone to bail me out today. The dollars will be there tomorrow, for sure.

W3. Today, I'm paying. After that, we'll see!

26

SEQUENCE VI

M1. I remember. I was sweating. I laughed while that guy, so carefully, was picking the splinters of glass out of my foot, one after the other. He handed me a cognac, had one himself. Blood was running down the sole of my foot, dripping on the mat. He taped me up. The jukebox, the Brazilian music. Someone was laughing. I asked for another cognac. And, limping, I went to the edge of the sea. I dropped on the sand. *The tide was rising.* I

W1. *The tide was rising.*
dropped. The arab started setting the umbrellas up in the sand, the black metal tables.

W1. *The tide was rising.*

M1. *The tide was rising.*

W1. The beach was a series of sandy rectangles, uniform, of identical texture, that the sea was erasing, unraveling at the edges. Concave, empty aluminum dinghies lay on the white water, hardly moving, perfectly reflected, without a shimmer. In each rectangle, the arab placed a mat, an umbrella, an iron table and an ashtray: pieces on a chessboard of sand.

M1. *We were heading toward each other, following the water's edge.*

W1. *We were heading toward each other, following the water's edge,* running, sprinkling ourselves, throwing rocks in the sea, taking photos. A publicity plane went by, the sea drug up empty bottles.

W2. Pour un bronzage magnifique, l'huile Ambre Solaire permet, développe un bronzage splendide et protège, nourrit et réhydrate la peau. Faire des applications à intervalle fréquent pendant l'exposition au soleil.

W1. He woke up with a start. He sat up. He fell back on the sand holding his bandaged foot. We helped him get back up. He told us about the accident, laughing. We took him to the bar, to have a drink. A tourist was staring at him. She ended up talking to him in German, about her apartments, her travels, I don't know what all. According to her, she spent

27

the year between New York, London and Paris. She was just coming from Istanbul, yes, I won't forget that detail. It was hot. The jukebox started another Brazilian record. Some boys were running toward the water, laughing, wrapped up in flowered towels. Their footprints erased the rectangles on the sand, crushing, distorting the edges, shifting the boundaries.

W1.   *They were laughing.*

M1.   *They were laughing.*

W1.   *Drunk no doubt.*

W2.   *Drunk no doubt.*

W1.   A glass broke.

W2.   Look. Look. Blood.

W1.   *A glass broke.*

M1.   *A glass broke.*

W1.   The cut on his foot. The splinters of glass. The red stains on the mat.

M1.   On the sand.

SEQUENCE VII

W2.   The Riviera (38a). Cannes by night. The quai St. Pierre and the Suquet. Realcolor. Mexichrome process.

W1.   We had decided to separate, like every year during the holidays, tired of our monotonous life, without complicity, without dialogue. We'd spent the day walking, without speaking, drinking in bars until we were smashed, killing time in the seedy waterfront cinemas: horror matinees in color. That night we started squabbling. We were eating in a restaurant on the beach, a little dazed by all that terror — «Opium and Flagellation in the Dock Districts» — I remember. I dropped a glass. A barefoot German who was passing near us stuck a splinter in his foot. A banal accident, but it led to apologies, interminable comments, which an exasperating touriste who was obviously interested in the victim came and meddled in; in the end, we had to have a round to make amends. Late that night, we left the German in that woman's arms and went on alone to our usual bars. The jukeboxes were repeating hit songs. They fell silent. Into the white, deserted alleyways that smelled of salt, onto posters pasted up, falling down, scraps of bright flophouse signs, battered cars and walls eaten away by saltpeter, spilled the reddish glow of the bars.

Farther on, the sea was streaked with the green, quick, lights of the smacks. On the yachts, in the port, the parties were over. The obese owners were fanning themselves, half-naked, stretched out in cane armchairs, shrieking with laughter, or trying to stagger over to the walkway to see off barefoot guests. Sailors were puking on the pier. The servants were carrying down cartons overflowing with scraps. Cats came running to rifle them.

W2.   Reflections of the Riviera. Monaco illuminated. The port, the Rainier III swimming pool and Monte-Carlo.

W1.   We went back to the hotel. The heat kept us from sleeping. We took the usual sleeping pills. No use. We decided to go back down on the beach. We walked along the sea. Day was coming on slowly, and the chill; we started talking again. We laughed.

W2.   Sound and Light of France. Cannes. Maritime Alps. Fisherman mending his nets, at the Port, near the quai St. Pierre.

W1.   We gathered stones; we started throwing them into the sea again. We ran. We had brought along the Instamatic, as usual. We were photographing everything: the water, the smacks, the advertising planes — which were already going by —, the blue, green and white succession of umbrellas corresponding to the different beaches. Suddenly, in front of the camera, an unexpected object appeared: on the sand, drunk no doubt, asleep, mouth open, blond, naked, tanned, lying on his back, feet covered by the tide, dissheveled, surrounded by flotsam, immobile, as if dead,
              a man was stretched out.

W2.   *a man was stretched out.*

M2. Everybody in! Everybody in!

M1. Cried the children. From the running group, like Roman standards, emerged swanshaped floats, wet suits, air mattresses, oxygen tanks, and harpoons. They clanked forward: enormous palmate paws of phosphorescent rubber.

M2. Everybody in! Everybody in!

M1. Called the pelican flock, tossing ice-cream cones on the sand. And then:

M2. A body! A body!

M1. They cried and leapt around the drunk blond. They made as if to gig him with their harpoons,

M2. to gut him to see what was in the body,

M1. to gouge out his eyes: I stopped them from dissecting him. An advertising plane went by: reading the streamer distracted them.

M2. So-much-fresh-er—So-much-fresh-er...

M1. They repeated, all the while sinking into the sea with their amphibious gear.

M3. We left without being noticed, quietly. We smiled to ourselves. I'd had a few drinks, a few drinks too many, I mean, in the company of a gaudy American. She kept talking about her apartments, the dear, and kept a hand on her green and black dollars. I staggered some maybe, walking.

M1. He put his arm around his neck. His breath stank of alcohol. We walked along the beach.

M2. Quite a way to make a living,

M1. I told him.

M3. One way like another to spend a vacation on the Riviera. Every pleasure has its price. So why not that one?

M2. He kissed my forehead.

M1. We were walking.

M2. His head on my shoulder.

M1. His head on my shoulder. We were walking. We were laughing. Behind us, in the distance, the Martians kept running in and out of the water, frenetic, beating each other with the harpoons, throwing handfulls of sand, squids wrapped up in little shining clouds.

M1. *We were laughing.*

M2. *We were laughing.*

M3. *We were laughing.*

M1. We went in the water. We swam. His drunkeness was gone: a new man.

M3. My passion,

M1. he said,

M3. is water-skiing, and parties in London with a little weed at the end.

M2. Actually, those two passions amount to one: to float in the transparent azur, to weigh no more, to fly, to glide, between colored discs, to breathe at last, in the silence.

M1. Psychedelic?

M2. His head on my shoulder.

M3. Psychedelic.

M2. Something like a flirtation of the soul with itself: to float, violet discs, intermittent, orange, enormous blue-fringed flowers, to sail, to become. Coolness. Silence. Water-skiing.

M1. *We were laughing.*

M2. *We were laughing.*

M3. *We were laughing.*

M2. And how about a coffee?

M3. I suggested.

M1. We went back toward the bar on the beach. We were walking in silence, going into the water from time to time, sprinkling ourselves, jostling each other. The wind was strong. The tide was rising. Groups of birds were coming off the sea, running in front of us on the beach, taking off again. We ran. You in front.

M3. Me in front.

M2. Me in front.

M3. You in front.

M1. We ran across the sand. We were nearing the bar. The Arab, I don't know why, no doubt because of the wind, was closing the umbrellas, laying them down, turning over the tables, folding the chairs. We ran. I was laughing. You cried out. I turned around. Halted on one foot, like a crane, you held up the other, bleeding. I started back toward you.

M3. I was sweating. I was laughing. (I wasn't going to lose face over a scratch!) Bastards!

M1. You had cut the sole of your foot on a harpoon. The blood fell onto the sand. People came from the bar, to see. The Arab brought a box of dressings, a cognac. A woman was about to faint. You were laughing.

M2. Perk up, man.

M3. you said to me.

M2. Now we're friends, eh? — you'll have to give me a cut rate.

M3. *We laughed.*

32

M1. *We laughed.*

M2. Then who had the idea of taking our picture?

M3. That American tourist, I remember. After all, it wasn't a bad idea; bright red always comes out well on an Instamatic.

SEQUENCE IX

W1. On your open hands, while you slept, fell the umbrella's orange shadow. On your palms, grains of obscurity, texture of the canvas, of the yellow circle, divided into zones of light varying with the stripes, more or less obscure, blue, your body abandoned to the absence of gestures, thickening in time, *measured by the water*

W2.   *measured by the water*

W2. I watch you sleep, falling deeper. Over my hands, almost imperceptible, passes a trembling, a twitch, hint of a gesture. They lay quiet again. Your closed eyelids tremble. Your lips part, half-open; for an instant, a slight crease wrinkles your forehead. Then your face becomes opaque again, inertia claims it, bit by bit, you give in, falling motionless, surrendered to your body's weight, to your heaviness against the sand. Among the shining grains, packed, still, grains of shadow outline a black oscillation, a letter perhaps, a gentle come and go, fading.

W1. I watched you sleep.

W2. You turn over. On the sand, concave, lurking, — absence — your body's imprint lingers. The wind wears it away, water fills the hollow left by your feet. You turn over.

W1. Farther on, there was an empty bottle, battered, of florescent plastic, with white letters.

W2. Farther on, a green and black line, with yellow edges, jagged, a seaweed perhaps.

W1. Farther on, a stone, a bird's timid step, a rotton oar, a rusty iron table, overturned.

W2.   Farther on, a child wrapped in a white towel, like an Arab horseman, or someone weeping over a tomb.

W1.   Farther on, under the bar's tent, crowded in, packed against each other, the members of an obese family, hyperwhite eunuchs crowned with flowered rubber bathing caps: placid, pale, smiling, stretched out in canvas armchairs — green stripes, pink volumes —. Massive muscles, irregular curve of the knees, cylindrical mass of the arms; the obese were laughing, applauding with their little bloated hands: a coke.

W1.   Farther on.

W2.   Farther on.

W1.   You were sleeping.

SEQUENCE X

M1.   The reefs emerged, reddish, surrounded with foam. The yacht was going by, slowly, near the beach, its beacons striking the shore. No one was left in the bars, on the sand. The night sent back our transistors' music, our conversations, already drunken, our laughter. The disc of yellow light revealed, signaled the things that slipped out of the shadow, magnified, burning, cutting, rapid, across the glowing circle, their ashen forms melting back into obscurity.

M1.   *A boat.*

M2.   *A boat.*

M1.   Fishermen were leaving the wharf: our beacon followed them. Blinded by the light, standing in the middle of their smacks, tossed by the waves, tangled in their nets, little men were jumping about and signaling us with their arms.

M1.   *We were laughing.*

M2.   *We were laughing.*

M1.   The brown reefs were reflected on the green stain of the sea, and on the

34

brown the ochre of the sand and on the ochre the white of the foam and on the white the orange of the moon and on the orange the changing blue of the waves.

M2. *Heat.*

W2. *Heat.*

M1. *We were singing.*

W1. *We were singing.*

M2. *Whiskey.*

W2. *Whiskey.*

M1. *We undressed.*

W1. *We undressed.*

M1. Hairy, with long beards, sitting on the sand, legs crossed, like four Tibetan monks, smoking — the cigarettes' red tips left grafitti in the air —, the musicians of a beat group officiated: flute, guitar, tambourine. The fourth lama — but we could hardly see — was clapping his hands to set the rhythm, singing perhaps. We shut off our transistors. Despite the distance, and covered at times by the sea, the music reached us. It was

M2. a Brazilian tune, sweet and monotonous, that developed without interruptions, without pauses, taking up the same theme, the same words maybe, as if it had never begun, as if, limitless, it would never end.

M1. Intermittence of music and light: we exchanged signals. Then they left the yellow disc, slipping away.

M1. *The sand again.*

M2. *The sand again.*

W1. *The empty disc.*

W2. *The empty disc.*

M1. *The silence.*

W1. *The silence.*

M1. We had skirted a good bit of the shore, still following the curve of the bay, still drinking, when a form appeared, on the sand, in the beacon's circle. Someone was stretched out, asleep, drunk, injured, drowned, at the very edge of the beach. Immobile, insensitive to the brutality of the light. Man? Woman?

W2. Dead? Alive?

M2. A body. Someone. At the center of the white halo. Immobile, turning. Rolling in the emptiness on a roof of sand. Caught, at the center of a halo, hands open.

W1. Dead? Alive?

W2. Drowned?

W1. We had turned off the lights inside the yacht. In the blackness, the dashboard was shining vaguely, the indicators, the green wheel of the tiller, the numbers a slow needle swept over. We fell silent: we heard the engine, the waves breaking against the prow, sometimes a helicopter, a bird, a cry on shore. The body, in the orange circle, would fall away, sway, exit, cut back in; just the head on the sand, the chest, then the entire body again. Now we were sure: it was a drunk woman, a drowned body the sea had washed up, an eccentric sleeping on the sand. We would find out about it in the morning papers.

Night was getting on. We decided to head back to the port. To make the trip again on shore, by foot. We had been living together for over a month, we were in love. We were living in a world of picture postcards. This had to be happiness, this forgetting of *watches,* and dates, this

W2.   *wonderful*

W1. *self-forgetting, this silence.*

W2. *splendid, magnificent.*

W1.   Everything was *wonderful, splendid, magnificent.* No, not

W2.   *wonderful, splendid, magnificent*

W1.   everything: his conversation was soporific, he wore thick glasses, he'd
      never heard of Joao Gilberto, and he didn't drink... but still, loving an
      archaeologist wasn't out of the question. On our return, on the pier, we
      decided to live together. We had to choose between his three flats, New
      York, Paris and London, all three, actually — I'd find out later —,
      identically filled with numbered stones, pieces of rusty metal, obsolete
      coins, German treatises and heads with broken noses. It was a perfectly
      managed summer romance, a Sagan scenario, a picture postcard.

W2.   A picture postcard.

W1.   Before leaving the yacht, we drank, or rather I made him drink, a glass
      of cold water with whiskey, and poured myself one, reversing the pro-
      portions. Day was coming on. We started walking along the shore. We
      would spend the day sleeping.
      (*we were in love*). I got used to these expeditions. The

W2.   (*we were in love*)
      summer solstice, I believe, made the sea ebb: he was able to discover am-
      phorae buried in old wrecks, still filled with wine, bronze statues or
      coins. We were searching
      (*we were in love*)

W1.   (*we were in love*)

W2.   Our finds were frequent, but they were pieces of squid
      tins, or tires, a fragment that said Shell, which is cute, we found stones
      that he judged to be worthless (they were all the same to me). *We were
      laughing.*

W1.   *We were*
      laughing.

M1.   *We were laughing.*

W1. *We were laughing.* We were running. We were taking photos. You did my portrait.

M2. You pulled an Ambre Solaire bottle out of the sand.

W1. An advertising plane was already going by in the sky.

W1. So much fresher.

W2. With the Express.

M1. *So much fresher.*

M2. *With the Express.*

W1. Suddenly, an unexpected object offered itself to our excavation mania. The woman we had seen from the yacht was still there. She was alive. She was dyed blond, or was wearing a wig. She didn't have the young, extraordinary body we had thought. A drunk teenager. We touched her. She woke up with a start.

W3. What time is it?

W1. She asked.

W2. What time is it?

W1. I asked at the same time.

W1. *We laughed.*

W2. *We laughed.*

W3. *We laughed.*

SEQUENCE XII

W3. A touch of freshness and youth on your face! Created for the young, Frost Lime Aqua Velva relieves razor sting, refreshes, tones up the skin.

Its subtle aroma evokes all the spicy freshness of green Carribean lemon, and distinguishes you from other men. Try it today. She'll let you know what she thinks!

M3. My compliments. You didn't have the slightest accent.

W3. I'm a call-girl.

M3. I asked for two whiskeys. I gave the waiter the usual sign: practically no water in her glass, and the opposite for me. She added: «So, the summer, and on the Riviera, one way like another to spend a vacation, waiting for the check I'm supposed to get for my latest film. When I have some money, I'll make love for love's sake.»

W3. In Paris five years.

M3. What film?

W3. «Opium and Flagellation in the Dock Districts».

M3. She added: «It's me you see nude, torturing the spy. Do you remember? With a black wig.»

W3. I start with one of his feet. He screams. Do you remember? I take a splinter of glass and cut him. Do you remember?

M3. I ordered two more whiskeys; no sign this time. Where shall we go?, I asked. I have three flats at my disposal, she said.

W3. You smell like fresh lemon.

M3. Hard to know whether this isn't more difficult work than other kinds. She added: «I'm a call-girl.»

W3. I've been living in Paris five years.

M3. She didn't have the slightest accent. And forward: «Are you offering me a whiskey?» We laughed. I took her picture. She wanted another one, nude: lights, Instamatic, action.

W3. *Très beau.*

M3. She added: «splendid, magnificent.» The tide was rising. I remember, she had a big gold chain around her neck, with thick links, and a Roman coin for a pendant.

W3. Found in the sea.

M3. She said. And she added:

W3. A gift from an archaeologist. A loaded American I spent a week on a yacht with. We had decided not to leave each other. We were in love.

M3. We laughed.

W3. *Let's make love.*

M3. *Let's make love.*

M3. It was a chance meeting. The night before, with my wife around, had been a nightmare. We had decided to separate, after spending a day in the bars around the docks, until we were smashed, in the cinemas, horror films over and over again, and then back into the bars. We had left each other at dawn. I had kept on walking along the shore, by the sea. I had thrown up. On the way back, I had discovered a blond woman asleep on the beach. I couldn't tell whether this immobile body, hardly breathing, as if dead, was or was not a creation of my drunkenness: I touched her. Touched her a second time. I wanted to convince myself that she was really alive, that she was really there.

W3. What time is it?

M3. She woke up with a start.

W3. *We laughed.*

M3. *We laughed.*

M3. I invited her to have a drink. *The tide was rising.*

W3.   *The tide was rising.* The Arab was setting up the umbrellas.

W3. The Arab was setting up the umbrellas, the iron tables.

M3. The Arab gave me the sign. He put us in an isolated corner of the bar. She didn't have the slightest accent. She told me very clearly: she was

W3. An actress in horror films, and

M3. during the summer, a call-girl.

W3. He smelled like lemon. I gave the waiter the usual sign. We had made a deal. I got a cut on each whiskey ordered. He poured soda in my glass, with a syrup that looked like whiskey. It's easy to do what you want with a drunk man. I saw right away that he had money. He spent the year between New York, Paris and London, and not in hotels either. I decided not to let him go.

M3. We asked for a second whiskey.

SEQUENCE XIII

W1. At first, I didn't notice anything. An exchange of gifts, between women, what could be more banal? She gave me

W2. an Indian shawl she had bought in London. I remember:

W1. It was a circle of white silk with 64 — we counted them — painted squares, forming a spiral into the central void, or out from it. On the gold in each square, six red brushstokes, long or short. The last square was the exact opposite of the first; there was no repetition.

W3. Well, anyway, keep it for yourself. A design that complicated gives me a headache. I thought I was buying a simple game of dominoes. Mathematics has always terrified me. Give me something of yours, as a memento, something you've liked.

W1. I didn't want to jump to conclusions. We had trouble understanding each other. She'd been in Paris for five months and had an awful German accent. She insisted on spending the night with me. I finally caught on when we went into this little club. There was hardly anyone there but women, and the few boys we met were pale, or had painted eyes: like disjointed wax dolls, on black felt divans. They were covered with dark, iron ornamentation, and Persian cats came rubbing up against them.

Shrouded by the smoke, some women with big studded-leather belts were drinking beer out of Bavarian mugs; green enamel bracelets, mouths open around a bifid tongue, coiled around their arms; the eyes were rubies.

We danced. Behind the walls, made of cloth panels lit at the angles, the band was hidden: Chinese shadows, spots of ink gesticulating in the white. Over a few Brazilian guitars, a flute was reproducing the arabesques of Joao Gilberto.

W1. *We felt each other's hair, and throat.*

W3. *We felt each other's hair, and throat.*

W1. *We felt our breasts cling together.*

W3. *We felt our breasts cling together.*

W2. The masks, on the divans, blond, immobile.

W1. We were euphoric. *Drunk perhaps.* We were laughing at everything.

W2.   *Drunk perhaps.*

W3. We were laughing at everything.

W1. *We were laughing at everything.*

W2. *We were laughing at everything.*

W1. You kissed my Indian shawl.

SEQUENCE XIV

W2. An enchanted universe: Cannes la nuit! Sound and Light at the Old Port, where the fishermens' dinghies seem to droop while their nets are drying, draped over long bamboo poles. And what more can be said about the palm tree, that wonderfully photogenic tree that makes Cannes Cannes! As the indispensable ornament of every beach, its elegance and «panache» have become part of the landscape's characteristic atmosphere. It satisfies our thirst for exotic charms and folklore. *At night, it lights up...*

W1.   *At night it lights up...*

M3. London? An asylum for drugged, filthy longhairs. Paris? Passé. Venice? A fief of the Guggenheims. New York? Devastated by the blacks. I'm bored stiff.

W1. It was the night before, after the daily conjugal scene (we had decided to separate), that I met him in a waterfront bar, where a Brazilian band had just opened. He offered me a whiskey.

W2. Me too, I'm bored.

W1. I told him.

W2. Fortunately there's still the cinema, art cinema I mean. Have you seen the latest one, «Opium and Flagellation in the Dock Districts»? Underground more underground than Warhol.

M3. I saw it, yes, of course, but I don't know where anymore. In New York, or in London, or...yes, at the Orly cinema, while I was waiting for a flight. I didn't see it all, I left in the middle of a good scene.

W2. You saw at least the Riviera sequence? It's the best one.

M3. The couple on the yacht, that one? Yes. I remember. The inside lights are out, they explore the coast with their beacon. On the screen, in turn, you see the yellow halo, then the dashboard, with phosphorescent numbers.

W2. That's it. Then in the following scene, they decide to go back, you see them landing at the pier. Then a quick shot, they're drinking whiskey, with a close-up on her hands, pouring the man's drink, and then her own. She's obviously trying to get the man smashed, and isn't drinking anything but water. Do you remember? Then there's a long pan: they're running on the pier; you hear Joao Gilberto on the soundtrack. They run one in front of the other. Her in front, then him, then her again. Behind them, you see an old city illuminated. A castle, I think, or

43

something like that, a lighthouse, a few yachts tied up at the pier. Do you remember?

M3.   No, I think I had to leave then.

W2.   Oh, that's terrible! The best scene is the next one. They're walking along the beach and suddenly a nude woman appears, asleep on the sand. Really extraordinary, like the woman turned to gold in Goldfinger. The camera roams over her body. They think she's dead. The man touches her. *Do you remember?*

W1.   *Do you remember?*

SEQUENCE XV

M1.   I don't remember. Why did we go back to the beach last night? We had forgotten something, the camera, I think, on the sand, we'd lost a key...

W1.   Maybe I'd lost my Indian shawl? No...that's stupid: I received the Indian shawl much later. I don't know. I don't remember anymore. We had come back to the beach, that's all. It was too hot at the hotel, maybe. Maybe we went to the bar.

M1.   I know we went as far as the bar on the beach, the one that stayed open all night. Yes...I can still see several details precisely. Everybody was smashed; a nude Arab, turbaned with a flowered towel, danced in the arms of a German blond, on the sand, to the sound of a small band of bearded Brazilians. People were photographing them with flashes. That, I haven't forgotten. I can still hear the music

M2.   moving continually, along with the bodies.

M1.   Why did we leave again? Why not stay there? Were we searching for something? Something lost, perhaps? *I don't remember.*

W1.   *I don't remember.*

M1.   I know we were walking barefoot, along the sea, moving away from the bar, and from the port. The sand was hard under our feet, compact, *black marble.* The line of foam gleamed an instant on

M2. *black marble*
this sinuous opacity, and then faded; lapping,
in the black

M2. *in the black*

M1. *of the water.*

M2. *of the water.*

M1. *Why were we moving away?*

W1. *Why were we moving away?*

M1. I don't know anymore. I know that a few smacks were half-sunk in the sand, broken, and that nothing was left of certain others but the frame, covered with seaweed perhaps, and rotting in the black water of the surf; on others, nets were stretched, whose mesh, white *in the night...*

M2. *in the night...*

W1. Were they sponge fishermen? *I don't remember anymore.*

W2. *I don't remember anymore.*

W1. They stayed close in to the shore, and lowered their lanterns into the water. Shining green.

W1. *The sea was receding.*

M1. *The sea was receding.*

M1. What were we searching for? I don't know anymore. A fisherman went by. He smelled of anisette. He was singing. He was walking barefoot.

W1. *A white bird went by.*

W2. *A white bird went by.*

M1. Another smack. All around, on the sand, as far as the reefs, a carpet of lichen, trapping empty, opened shells, broken bottle ends, and baskets of gutted oysters.

M2.   *Silence.*

W2.   *Silence.*

M1.   I don't remember.

M2.   *An odor of iodine, of salt.*

W2.   *An odor of iodine, of salt.*

M1.   We advanced carefully. Through the rubble of shells and splinters of glass. On the other side of the smack we found clean sand again. We let ourselves drop, tired. Not wanting to come back.

W2.   Why not sleep here?

M1.   *The sea was receding*

W1.   *Black.*

W1.   We lay down. Next to one another.

M2.   One without the other. Your shirt open.

M1.   I felt the water against my feet; your body against mine.

M1.   *On the sand.*

M2.   *On the sand.*

M2.   *Black.*

W2.   *Black.*

M1.   We separated. I remember. Someone was coming.

W2.   Someone.

W1.   A man, a woman?

M1.   A man, a woman?

W1. Someone was coming.

M1. It was a thin woman, young perhaps, certainly blond. She went by rapidly, her gaze turned toward the sea. Without speaking to us. Without turning around.

W1. She moved away.

M1. *Over the black sand.*

M2. *Over the black sand.*

M1. We drew closer.

W2. *You and me.*

M2. *Again.*

M1. The fishermen were returning.

W1. And the lanterns,

W2. green,

M1. in the water. Silence.

M1. *The fishermen were returning.*

M2. *And the lanterns,*

W1. *green,*

W2. *in the water. Silence.*

SEQUENCE XVI

W3. I know: that's called narcissism. Makes no difference to me. «Those who reproach Narcissus lack the means to approach him.» I had seen my film for the umpteenth time, I admit. Every time it's billed, I go into the cinema. I know it by heart, but I don't get tired of it; I wait for the moment when my image will unfold on the screen, speak with my mouth, move with my body. I like to think I change: sometimes I'm prettier, sometimes the color of my eyes changes, or else I've aged. I prefer different scenes every time: some days, the torture one — when they stick splinters of glass in my foot — seems terrific, on other days it seems like a cheap imitation of James Bond, and I prefer the meeting with the man on the beach, when I touch him to see if he's alive, and he sits up, and we both laugh.

But tonight seeing my film kind of depressed me. It was in a little, broken-down, dirty neighborhood cinema, that stank of dust and disinfectant. The sound was out during the credits; the film broke a number of times — once during the torture scene, as a matter of fact. I left before the end: no point in waiting for the scene in black and white, the projection was so bad it was sure to be a fiasco.

I walked around the docks, which is no stroll for a woman alone, and blond, in these parts. The placard of a little club caught my attention. A reddish glow was spilling into a white alleyway, with walls eaten away by saltpeter. A Brazilian band was introduced. I went straight in. My second deception wasn't long coming. It was one of these chic little clubs where no one dances and the musicians are bored. The men, alone at the bar, overdressed, were draining huge mugs of beer, and talking politics and horses; the women were yawning, pale, suffocating from the heat, sunk back into black felt divans with their cats. The only bearable thing there was the band, set up in front of a cloth screen, but even that for no more than an hour; after a while, the music was sugary and monotonous. I had a few drinks alone and decided to go back out. I walked along the St. Pierre pier, watching the insipid yacht owners, alone in their deluxe tin cans, rocking in front of a television screen, hoping a success would bring them ultimate bliss. I was walking at the edge of the water, barefoot, without the least desire to go back to the hotel, drunk perhaps. Night was getting on. Suddenly I stopped: right there, on the sand, two bodies. It wasn't a couple making love: they were separated, immobile. You would have said two drowned bodies washed up by the sea. I came closer. Were they breathing? Dead or alive? I was worn out. I shook them. They jumped up. I didn't know what to say.

W2. What time is it?

W3. asked the woman, after a silence. I don't know.

W1. She said to me.

W3. Excuse me...I thought...

W2. That's alright. We were lying down after having had a few too many drinks. Can't sleep in a yacht when the tide's strong. How about you, you're not sleeping?

M1. I asked her.

W3. I was going to sleep.

M2. Do you know where we can get a cup of coffee?

W3. At the bar on the beach, over there, it stays open all night.

M2. Come along with us, since you're headed in that direction.

M1. I told her.

W3. Fine.

W1. We walked.

W3. She didn't have the slightest accent.

M1. We walked.

W3. No sooner did we get to the bar, than they ran into one of their friends. He was one of these bored Americans who drink all night, till they drop. The coffee was transformed into a watered-down whiskey. Obviously, the American was interested in me.

M3. I've seen you somewhere before, I think. I'm sure of it...but I don't know where. The face — I know I've seen it somewhere before.

W3. He was watching me closely.

M3. I always have trouble, when I recognize someone, figuring out when and where I saw them the first time. Paris? London? New York?

W3. Perhaps.

W1. We laughed.

W3.   The American had drunk too much. He was stuttering. He could hardly control his movements. We got up to leave. He was trying to get up to see us off when he dropped his glass. The puddle of whiskey sparkled a moment on the floor, with the pieces of glass.

W1.   Then we realized we'd gotten splinters of glass stuck in our feet.

W3.   I looked at mine. I didn't have any.

M1.   I had picked the glass out of your foot, carefully, and then out of mine. A trickle of blood ran across the skin, fell onto the mat and grew, forming a dark stain, almost black.

W3.   I was afraid I'd faint. I asked for a cognac.

M1.   The Arab came up, with a broom and a dustpan, to clean up the pieces. We asked him for some bandages. He brought us two old pieces of sticking plaster, which was enough.

W1.   Now we looked like two invalids; two herons. We were walking arm in arm, each on one foot.

W3.   *We were laughing.*

M1.   *We were laughing.*

W1.   Striding along, we went as far as the edge of the water. There, we let ourselves drop, from sleep and fatigue.

W3.   The American left. He wanted to take me with him on his yacht. I accepted. Everything was sad and grey on the beach. The couple were sleeping; they were lying on one another, like they were making love.

M1.   I remember; a dream scene: I was walking in a greenhouse, down a corridor lit by an icy, white light, I was crushing soft, slimy plants, molluscs. I listened to the murmur of sprouting orchids. There were strange, black-striped animals in vertical aquariums, open like flowers surrounded with phosphorescent flagellae. Far away, I heard music — Indian? Suddenly, striding over a carpet of moss, I felt a burning in my foot. I'd stepped on a sea-urchin, or a sharp, open shell, something with a blade. I don't know. I was bleeding.

W1. I woke up. The Arab was coming, umbrellas folded up under his arms, and was setting them up one after the other in the rectangles of sand.

W2. In the rectangles of sand, the Arab was setting up the umbrellas.

M2. The black metal tables, *on the sand.*

W3. *on the sand.*

SEQUENCE XVII

W1. In the white light of morning, the colors were evaporating, the forms were dissolving, everything was decomposing, everything was revealed.

M1. The sky stretched taut; the trails, already, of rattling single prop planes.

W2. Stuyvesant.

M2. Happy Holidays.

M1. *Now, I remember.*

W1. *Now, I remember.*

M1. Very precisely.

W1. Very precisely.

W1. Too much so. A millemetric picture.

M1. sharp,

W2. blinding,

M1. of drugs.

M2. Blue.

W2. Bazile, Gigou, Dufy.

M2.   Blue.

M1.   Brown.

W2.   Green.

M3.   Brown.

W3.   White.

W1.   Red.

M1.   Do you remember?

W1.   Do you remember?

M2.   The umbrellas, *all along the beach,* still fringes, circles.

M1.   *all along the beach*

M2.   canvas, *on the moving fringe of the water.* From the fringe water, white.

W1.   *on the moving fringe of the water*

M2.   *moving on the sand,* advancing, receding,

W2.   *moving on the sand*

M2.   still for an instant and then back *under the row of circles;*

M3.   *under the row of circles*

M2.   the water spreads out, striped by *the trail of the smacks,* wake of foam...

W3.   *the trail of the smacks*

W2.   ...on the water, *whiter than the sand,* fading, erased, written

W1.   *whiter than the sand*

W2.   *on the canvas,*

52

M1. *on the canvas,*

W2. still, caught by the Instamatic, you remember. *Do you remember?*

M3.   *Do you remember?*

W2. I went on.

W3. I went on.

SEQUENCE XVIII

M1. The river, the frost, the margins covered with carpets of thick, somber signs *the open sea,* washing up voices, the apples floating

M2.   *obscure signs*

M1. near the shore, *nearer,* farther, writing on the sand

W1.   *near the shore*

M1. always *the same text,*

W2.   *over the sand*

M1. ran the river, the frost, the water would erase them, had already erased the textures, *the frozen river* with margins of white stone

M3.   *the textures*

M1. covered with mauve carpets; *the open sea*, washing up

W3.   *mauve carpets*

M1. the voices, the apples floating near the shore, nearer, farther, on the sand, always writing *the same signs...*

M2.   *on the sand*

M2. On the sand always writing *the same text,* the book of books

W1.   *the book*

M2. *describing a face,* the water would erase it, had already

W2. *erased the textures*

M2. erased the textures. Then the *last thaws* meet, and

M3.   *green stones, birds*

M2. roll, trailing green stones, birds, the murmur behind *the mountain at night,* until the river, the frost

W3. *the river, the frost*

M2. *margins overgrown* with carpets of thick, somber signs...

W1. *somber signs*

W1. Thick somber signs, *the open sea* washing up

W2.   *the apples*

M1.   *nearer*

W1. voices, and the apples floating near the shore, *nearer,* farther

M2.   *farther*

W3.   *the textures*

W1. on the sand always writing the same text, the water will erase *the textures* there, barely visible

M3. *uncertain edge*

W2. *mauve plain*

W1. on the uncertain edge of the *mauve plain,* separated

W2.   *spots of salt*

M1.	*a dead fish*

W1. sometimes by spots of salt, by a dead fish...

W2. On the line, the frost, the mouth, stretched between the margins overgrown with carpets *of thick somber signs,*

M1.	*open sea*
M2.	*the apples*
W3.	*farther*

W2. far from the open sea, washing up the voices, the apples floating near the shore, nearer, farther, that are always writing on the sand, *the same text.*

M3. *the textures*

M1. *obscure signs*

M2. *the voices*

W2. The water will erase the textures, will form the delta of a river, of a frost, with margins overgrown with carpets, thick somber signs, and the open sea washing up the voices...

M3. The golden apples, summits of *shifting triangles,*

M2.	*shadows*
M2.	*rock bottom*
W1.	*in the ice*
W2.	*the river*

M3. shadows on the rock bottom, trapped in the river's ice...

W3. Between the black line of the *margins* overgrown with

M1.	*carpets*

M2.   *thick signs*

W1.   *somber*

W2.   *the open sea*

W3. carpets of thick somber signs and the open sea.

M1. *and the open sea.*

M2. *and the open sea.*

W1. *and the open sea.*

W2. *and the open sea.*

M3. *and the open sea.*

W3. *and the open sea.*

FALL:
BARROCO FUNERARIO

NOTE

Translator's note: The Spanish title of *Fall* is *La Caída*, a term which carries a general sense of «collapse» or «ruin»; other usages signify a prostitute's pay and «witty remarks» or repartee, as well as the radiophonic sense of «clips» referred to in note 1. While the English *clips* has the advantage of signifying both «to cut apart» and «separate» as well as «to put together,» it of course lacks the thematic resonance of *caída* or *fall*; the reader should bear in mind, then, that *clips* is used here to designate the tape montage which both separates and connects the sequences, articulating their differences in a plural, heterogeneous ensemble.

1. The term *caída* (fall/clip) has been taken here in that sense, among others, which is used in radio jargon: a fragment of rejected, residual tape which is eliminated from the definitive version. These fragments, which ordinarily collect on the studio floor, will be used here in the indicated places, as the «clips» which terminate each sequence. The producer should construct an auditory phrase, either by splicing the clips together mechanically or by cutting, folding or replaying them at a different speed, and by amplifying them through an echo chamber; with these fragments as raw material, he begins to write *his* play.

2. As the play progresses, the six voices cite fragments of the text which they deliver at other moments, preceding or following. These citations are to be integrated into the rhythm of the sequence in such a way as to become *verbal*, but not *tonal*, grafts. In this version of the play, we have chosen for each citation that sentence which corresponds best — which clashes the least — with the thematic development of the sequence.

The actors may, if they wish, replace the cited sentence with another drawn from the same text. They may also exclude the citation, or add a sentence of their own invention, summarizing, clarifying, judging, commentating on or parodying the «dramatic situation.» Or finally, while retaining the citation proposed by the author, they may add another of their own invention. In brief, an attempt to eliminate the passive notion of actor-interpreter; the actor must pass through the «other» side of the work, to participate in or challenge it as he re-emerges at the moment of it genesis.

The texts from which to borrow the citations carry the label *TEXT*; the cited texts are placed to the right-hand side of the page and carry the label *(citation)*. The *TEXT*s correspond to the sequences with the same number.

3. Voices 1, 3 and 5 are masculine; voices 2, 4 and 6 feminine. These might be considered as actually being two characters, the one female and the other male.

4. The word *gallery* is given in several senses here, deriving primarily from the Italian usage: a covered passage, catacomb, place where paintings are exhibited, tunnel, etc.

5. *Fall* may be considered as the succession of six developments emerging from the same *generator*: a flower-bed (in the French pun, «parterre de capucines,» *capucin(e)* designating at one a monk, nun, nasturtium or pigeon. — Tr.) within a covered space *(gallery)*, an inanimate body beneath it.

This «parterre de capucines» alludes to the carpet of remains which covers the floor of the famous catacombs at Palermo; but also to a well-known flowered carpet of the same name — Sartre played on this analogy — and in addition, to a flowered bedspread; to a decorative rug with quilted flowers, etc. The reign of the inanimate goes from imitation — the game, the parody — to dreams, and to death.

6. The «clacker» toy described as the play opens, which was popular a few summers ago in Italy, and which is probably of Chinese origin, intervenes here as the sonic form of repetition, of obsession: mechanical life next to the inanimate. The shape which the small sphere trace in the air — a parenthesis — illustrates the text's citational structure: the citations are so many repetitive parentheses in the latter's development.

7. *Fall* is the reverse side of *The Beach*: instead of the body apotheosized and eroticism, the body degraded and death.

8. *Fall:* a parenthesis around the *(a)bject;* to indicate, in the image of the clacker, the *panse* (dressing for a wound, a patch, a stop-gap — Tr.) of the Lacanian object (a).

SEQUENCE ONE

VOICE ONE, TEXT ONE

«Clackers,» also known as «nut-crackers» or the «chatter-box»: two plastic spherules, smaller than eggs, hung at the ends of a thick string; the median point is a ring. With each vertical motion of the hand, the spheres collide, rebound, and collide again with a crisp smack. A quick motion makes them collide above and below, at the points that would coincide with the XII and the VI on a clockface.

VOICE TWO, TEXT ONE

All along the gallery, formed by the eaves of the cabins, children — with large heads and very clear oval eyes — were playing, in bathing suits. Around their little, rubbery, mustard-colored, clasped hands, the spheres left fluorescent circles in the greyish air, which overlapped, fragmented, faded, bit by bit, until they vanished; flowing, milky rings, white against the white of the night.

VOICE THREE, TEXT ONE

All of the doors and windows were open. All along the gallery, the interiors appeared one after another: tiny rooms, crowded with old furniture; around the lamp-shades' wavering, whitish light, like insects attracted by some florid glare, the guardians' families were crowding in. In the center, a large unmade bed; an old man, seated, surrounded by cushions, fans himself, coughs. On the night-table, among flasks and spoons, a fan. Another fan on the ceiling, still, like a lamp; its black blades are covered with flies. A cradle. Pink celluloid rattles on the mosquito netting of white tulle, with silk knots.

V4. Other children were passing by, running; baggy trousers, starched shirts, short sleeves, hair neatly parted; they had sticks in their hands, and were pushing a hoop; at their wrists, cuff-links with small stones; on their collars, docile black butterflies.

V6. At the end of the gallery, several of them were standing together: silent, motionless, they kept shaking their toys, and pointing their left hands toward the interior of one of the little houses.

V2. Strong wind.

V1. We could hear the whistle of a train, farther on.

VOICE FOUR, TEXT ONE
Next to a pantry — loaves wrapped in white linen, pitchers of wine — on a narrow table with long, curling legs, a phonograph with a large horn and crank-handle; we heard the voice of a tenor on the final notes of a well-known aria, as if through a cube of tin.

V4. The table is set. The silver-drawer open, gaping.

V6. The sugar bowl overturned on the tablecloth.

V3. The white spot of sugar shone in the light of a copper lamp whose volutes open onto glass knobs.

VOICE FIVE, TEXT ONE
A bluish glow was emanating from a television set, but there was no sound or picture, — only a trembling neon daylight that barely lit the room.

V6. Following the children's imperative fingers — each had his own hoop, and one was smoking — we entered cautiously.

VOICE SIX, TEXT ONE
The bed was made: the quilt was embroidered with tiny yellow flowers. With her shoes on, a little girl was lying on her back, with her head at the edge of the bed, as if asleep.

V3. A diffuse glow, filtered by an embroidered curtain, cast a spot on her body.

V2. Satin shoes on her feet.

V4. Two thick cords ran from her rigid hands; hung at their ends, joined, two metal balls were shining.

V6. Against the end wall, in an urn, among the tin hearts and bellies, a plaster virgin crowded with tiny colored phials, wax flowers in faintly colored vases.

V2. Tapers trembling in red glass saucers.

V4. A small tube of neon — squared, with one corner left open — frames the urn.

(CLICK-CLACK)

V6. They hadn't been playing at poison, but at doctor, bambini piccoli. They had used up all the pills and potions. Exhausted, out of ideas, they tried sugar-water. They'd found a packet at the bottom of a flask, dissolved it in some milk, and administered this other sugar to the patient.

V4. They hadn't been playing at poison.

V3. They repeated,

V4. at bambini piccoli,

V2. and they started up their clackers all at once.

> *Voice three, text one (citation):*
> All of the doors and windows were open.

V1. The children — with their wide, yellow eyes — were watching us defiantly.

V2. The smallest one was wearing a topper; a gold chain hung from a buckle on his pants; a watch was swinging on the end; on the lid, two initials.

V4. Between his arms, a cat with pink fur and urine-colored eyes was watching us.

V2. Another, curled up in a chair, was contemplating the little girl's feet.

V6. The largest of the children, a little fat, rings under his eyes, sallow-skinned, dressed in a black frock-coat with a starched tail dangling motionless, was sporting a stuffed frog in his breast pocket, as if it were a silk handkerchief: feet splayed open, with small suckers at the fingertips.

> *Voice six, text one (citation):*
> The bed was made: the quilt was embroidered with tiny yellow flowers.

V3.   A carpet of flowers, with a border of shining fringes, shaken by the wind.

V4.   Hot, sandy gusts were coming in through the doors and windows, from the sirocco.

V2.   Against the zinc eaves, the wind's whistling continues.

V2.   Against the zinc eaves, the wind's whistling continues.

V3.   The shutters were opening and slamming shut.

V4.   Farther on, the sea,

V6.   the birds,

V2.   the whistle of a train,

V1.   At the end of the gallery,

V3.   on the carpet of flowers,

V5.   the body in white.

(CLICK-CLACK)

CLIPS

SEQUENCE TWO

VOICE ONE, TEXT TWO
Tossed upward from little half-developed hands, the ball leaves a fiery trace in the air; as if space conserved the drawing of things. The objects are formed of layers, closed with lines that continue on, beyond, to the limits of the canvas.

VOICE TWO, TEXT TWO
In the second room, a red circle. Two small, white, symmetrical spheres are following its edges, joined in the center by spokes just as white. The small spheres meet at the top of the circle, at the point that would coincide with the XII on a clockface, and then

> *Voice four, text four (citation):*
> they begin a slow descent, tracing two sym-
> metrical curves through the air, a magnetic
> parenthesis, drawn back down, slowly, slowly,
> to collide with a crisp smack, a clack, a toy's
> click, a metallic bird's flutter.

V2. At the lowest point, the one that would correspond to the VI on a
clockface, the two spherules are still for an instant, and then start the
same path upwards again.

VOICE THREE, TEXT TWO
In the next room, rather than hanging canvases, the artist has preferred to
recreate an ambiance where we become the subjects, as soon as we enter: a
small-town American bar, furnished in the style of the forties.

V6. In the center of the room, which is lined with a wall-paper pattern of
pale dahlias, a blues record is playing on a juke-box with flashing lights.

VOICE FOUR, TEXT TWO
Another reconstruction by the same artist: the interior of a working-class
Mediterranean home; curving furniture, with stained, broken, leaf-work
molding.

> *Voice two, text five (citation):*
> Old rubbish found in pawn shops, disjointed
> furniture, the ornaments of a funeral baroque,
> set into the walls rather than hung.

V1. On the night-table, a portrait, with flowers.

> *Voice four, text one (citation):*
> Next to a pantry, on a narrow table with long,
> curling legs, a phonograph with a crank-handle
> and large horn. As if through a cube of tin, we
> heard

V2. the voice of Caruso.

V4. Against the end wall, an urn.

V5. An empty room next. No canvases, no sculpture. Just a tape-recorder

65

playing on a table and a few photos stuck to the wall; or perhaps the same image, only with imperceptible variations; a postage stamp pasted to each one.

V3.   Theater photos. More than the postures of the six characters — one of them a priest —, without affectation or posing, without make-up or period costumes, what indicated the theatrical nature of the meeting, what denounced its representation, was the decor: a reconstruction, quite obviously made of cardboard, of the famous catacombs at Palermo.

VOICE FIVE, TEXT TWO
The tape that was playing confirmed this conjecture: a play had been recorded, or rather its rehearsals; the repetitions gave it away, the actors' emphatic tone, the studied simplicity of the text, and even that familiar echo that footsteps have on the boards of a stage.

VOICE SIX, TEXT TWO
The floor of the last room is covered over with a green grass of polyester fibers. Small pale brown flowers, dotting the painted rubber at regular intervals, in a cross-hatch pattern. Prone, with closed fists, holding something, a plaster cast of a female form, roughly sculpted, lies in one of the carpet's angles, faceless.

V4.   The grass glows, lit by the play of some spots.

V6.   The reflection colors the walls,

V2.   the statue of plaster.

(CLICK-CLACK)

V1.   At the end of the gallery,

V3.   on the carpet of flowers,

V5.   the body in white.

(Far away; the sea, the birds, the whistle of a train.)

CLIPS

SEQUENCE THREE

VOICE ONE, TEXT THREE
Not without punctilio, a mannered monk was guiding us along the gallery, which here and there was lit by lancets glassed over with thick yellow panes: pigeons lit on them, darkening them. On the worn, white flagstones, with no apparent joints, a ring of mustard light edged on with the day, crossed by the shadows of wings.

V1. Around the garret windows, tibias and femurs carpeted the vaults in regular circles.

V2. Skull-caps were wedged in where the ribs crossed.

V3. In the joints between the stones, small, broken bones were mixed with the cement; crushed, transformed into powder, they covered the catacomb; granules of another white, lime on the limestone.

VOICE TWO, TEXT THREE
Standing, leaning against the walls, seated before rough pulpits of nailed planks, dipping goose plumes in dry inkwells, attentive still to the trace of a gold initial, sometimes kneeling, stacked in the corners, or even balancing lightly on top of the beams, thousands of skeletons observed their tasks with empty gestures, meticulous, exemplary, arranged by the capuchins all along the catacomb, and the centuries, each according to his office, in rigorous confraternity.

V3. Encircling the phalanges, an embroidered chasuble.

V5. A monstrance between two wrists, pressed against a fissured sternum.

V1. A mitre slipping on a skull.

V2. Hard at work, «the two companions» are deciphering a missal, their eye-sockets empty.

V2. On a panel set into the wall at the point where the different strips of molding meet, the monk who is guiding us presses a lever

            Voice one, text two (citation):
            which leaves a fiery trace in the air; as if space

67

conserved the drawing of things.

VOICE THREE, TEXT THREE
On the front of an empty altar, covered with dust, at the foot of a niche where a decapitated statue and censer lay abandoned, a rectangle of neon flashes and then lights up:

> *Voice five, text one (citation):*
> a bluish glow was emanating from it — a trembling neon daylight that barely lit the cavern.

VOICE FOUR, TEXT THREE
On a black velvet shroud, embroidered with Moorish fretwork, the yellowed silk of a dress appears: a faded pelerine, an irregular sparkle of brooches, the waxy face, carefully combed, of an embalmed girl holding a doll against her breast, the same color she is. Alone, among all the bones, her flesh stretched taut.

VOICE FIVE, TEXT THREE
Locks of hair, reliquaries, engravings and portraits adorn the thick glass of her shrine.

VOICE SIX, TEXT THREE
A name between two indistinct dates; the shrine among the paper flowers.

V4. Bambina Rosalia Lombardo.

V6. Born in nineteen...

V2. eighteen, perhaps.

V3. Died in nineteen...

V4. twenty, perhaps twenty-one.

V2. Embalmed by the monks.

V4. With her wooden toys.

V6. With her dolls and her cats.

(CLICK-CLACK)

V1. Saved from the beasts.

V3. — explained the monk,

V1. from the ravenous clamor of the earth!

V3. Hamming, he added after a silence:

V1. No, this angel did not deserve to become the diet of worms!

V3. When a few moments had passed, he turned off the neon rectangle.

V1. And with this relic, gentlemen,

V3. — he opens his mouth ostentatiously on the vowels, like a singer —,

V1. our path through this meadow of remains, mute emblems of human transience, comes to an end. Of kings and nobles, of saints and bishops, of pomp and power, only this remains: coarse and gruesome ornaments, white splinters in the cement which binds the stones, a dust that cloaks these walls with a new layer of lime.

V3. An octagonal chapel, covered with latten arms, crutches, golden eyes and miniature crystal tubes filled with ashes, interrupted the gallery. A spiral staircase mounted from there toward a trap-door whose cracks let through the sunlight.

V1. This way

V3. — said the monk as he pointed to the stairs.

Voice five, text two (citation):
With an actor's emphatic tone.

V3. He took up his post near the first step, waiting for his tip: smiling.

V1. Gentlemen,

V3. — he concludes brusquely —

V1. our visit is over.

V3. He pocketed the coins. And began his ascension,

V2. up the spiral staircase.

V4. Multiplied by the gallery's echo,

V6. his ascent resounded.

> *Voice five, text two (citation):*
> With that familiar echo that footsteps have on
> the boards of a stage.

V2. We turned back one last time, before leaving the gallery,

> *Voice one, text three (citation):*
> which here and there was lit by lancets glassed
> over with thick yellow panes; pigeons lit on
> them, darkening them.

V4. The remains,

> *Voice two, text three (citation):*
> arranged by the capuchins all along the
> catacomb, and the centuries,

V4. on the floor

> *Voice one, text three (citation):*
> of worn, white flagstones, with no apparent
> joints,

V4. forming a carpet of bone flowers.

> (The voice of Caruso)

V4. White garden

V6. under the mustard light,

V2. crossed by the shadows of wings.

V1.   And at the end of the gallery,

V3.   on the carpet of flowers,

V5.   the body in white.

(CLICK-CLACK)

CLIPS

SEQUENCE FOUR

VOICE ONE, TEXT FOUR
And then everything comes together very slowly, but with no hesitation, no slips: as if the entire sequence had been perfectly learned, rehearsed, and programmed, instant after instant, as if each motion conformed to a memorized key, to a code the actors were following silently. Or, rather than actors, figurines pulling strings, manikin cut-outs in the shadow-theater.

V2.   Very slowly: the body sluggish,

V4.   the air's resistence.

V3.   Very slowly. Each of the characters seems to calculate his gestures — wary, or timid — and execute them cautiously, as if one pace quicker than another might raise a cloud of dust, reverberate into the distance, onto another surface, unleashing some danger.

(CLICK-CLACK)

V5.   It's dark. We're seated on the terrace of a café. The square, paved with great, convex, porous stones, is built on a sloping plane. Through the interstices of umbrellas with thick green stripes we can see the broken volutes of a facade, illuminated by spotlights: acanthus leaves, shields, garlands encrusted with nitre, cherubim.

V3.   The pediment is a triangle with broken sides.

V5.   Attracted and blinded by the spotlights, a peacock waddles up and stops at the base.

V3.   In the center of the square, the village boys are watching us: red velveteen pants, spindly legs. Shirts open: on their chests, large black coins.

V2.   Others are going by on motorcycles. The sound of brakes, a network of tangled traces. The tires leave a fanshaped design singed across the stones.

(CLICK-CLACK)

V5.   We head down to the bottom of the square. Very slowly. We can feel it, we're being watched. The angles of a staircase, made from bits of sculpture, old chased medallions, torn from the façade perhaps.

V6.   Inside squares with rounded angles, that have lost their relief, worn by the footsteps: two fish, parallel, heading in opposite directions, biting the same line; two small, identical men; a scorpion. In a step of pink clay, the stump of a marble arm.

VOICE TWO, TEXT FOUR
From the top of the hill, looking out over the street, we could make out the salt-marsh basins near the sea, crowded like animals around a trough, closed off and cross-hatched with black earthwalls. Glittering railroad tracks crossed them. Birds were tracing spirals as they flew.

V1.   The village was deserted.

V5.   We went down a street.

V2.   Through the white-curtained windows, filtered by lace flowers, the tacky gleam and perpetual whine of television screens.

V5.   We were about to head back up to the square, when a gang of children appeared in front of us, furiously shaking their clackers.

> *Voice two, text one (citation):*
> They had large heads, very clear oval eyes. Around their little, rubbery, mustard-colored, clasped hands, the spheres left flourescent circles in the greyish air, which overlapped, fragmented, faded bit by bit until they vanished: flowing, milky rings, white against the white of the night.

V5. They kept clicking their toys, and with their left hands waved us toward a sculpted doorway, crowned by broken shields and a stone trinacria.

V6. The door opened onto the gallery of a cloister with Norman arcades. Columns with minute, geometrical insets, star-shaped polygons dividing on the red stone, green and golden arabesques.

> *Voice six, text six (citation)* –
> Torches that would not die out soon

V4. were lighting a stone fountain.

V2. At the end of the cloister, a stairway began, its steps covered with potted flowers. Tiny vases of red riverclay were hung from the balustrade around the upper level.

V4. Very fine mashrabiyyah work screened the windows.

V5. Flowers like the ones decorating the balcony, but livelier, with more intense colors, were sprouting from the ground, in the interstices between the stones; a uniform bed of bursting monkshood, the entire length of the cloister and the gallery that bordered it.

(CLICK-CLACK)

VOICE THREE, TEXT FOUR
On the carpet, leaning against a column, a little girl was seated at the end of the gallery.

V5. Dressed in tulle.

V1. With long hair.

V3. White under the moon.

V4. We came up to her.

V2. She was surrounded by her wooden toys.

V4. With a doll the same color she was.

V6.   Curled at her feet, sticking out their tongues, two cats with pink fur, with urine-colored eyes, were watching us.

V3.   Haughty. In her right hand, like an allegory of Justice, she held up two shining spherules hanging at the ends of an elastic cord which, very slowly, as if endowed with unlike forces, repelled one another, then moved away from the horizontal, rejoining once more at the top of the path they had just traced.

VOICE FOUR, TEXT FOUR
Once at this height they stopped for an instant, and then began a slow descent, tracing two symmetrical curves through the air, a magnetic parenthesis, drawn back down, slowly, slowly, to collide with a crisp smack, a clack, a toy's click, a metallic bird's flutter.

V2.   Very white hands.

V4.   Satin shoes.

V6.   Black hair falling to the waist, that held dragonfly brooches, cameos, ribbons of silk,

> *Voice two, text five (citation):*
> the ornaments of a funereal baroque.

VOICE FIVE, TEXT FOUR
On the capitals, coranic script, twining animals.

VOICE SIX, TEXT FOUR
In the dark, the mosaics glittered on the columns.

V4.   Behind the mashrabiyyah,

V6.   severe eyes

V2.   were watching us.

V1.   At the end of the gallery,

V3.   on the carpet of flowers,

V5.   the body in white.

(Voices multiplied by a gallery's echo, the familiar echo that footsteps have on the boards of a stage.)

CLIPS

SEQUENCE FIVE

VOICE ONE, TEXT FIVE
The next chapter is altogether different. The sentences are short and seemingly careless. The narrative doesn't advance; or rather, it advances around the margins, through forms without visible connection to the central image or theme.

V2.   Describing two canvases — one by Cremonini, the other by Ado —, an exhibition of conceptual art by David Lamelas, a carpet by Martial Raysse and one of Segal's sculptures.

VOICE TWO, TEXT FIVE
The author stands for a long time in one of those accumulated «settings» that Kienholz composes: old rubbish found in pawn shops, disjointed furniture, the ornaments of a funereal baroque, set into the walls rather than hung.

VOICE THREE, TEXT FIVE
An old yellow carpet, obviously home-woven, covers the floor with little flowers that must have been a bright, gaudy red;

> *Voice two, text five (citation):*
> set into the walls
>
> *Voice one, text four (citation):*
> Manikin cut-outs in the shadow-theater.

VOICE FOUR, TEXT FIVE
A large radio set, in varnished wood, broadcasts a dialogue with no direct relation to the decor, without any evident articulation whatsoever with what we see around us; the voices are all young, for instance, even though it looks like only old people live in this hovel.

(Fragments of this same sequence are heard in the background, beginning with «Voice five, text five.»)

V2. The dialogue is not about poverty, nor old age or madness, and yet something more subtle, only barely perceptible, places the voices within this same «setting», this setting we became characters in as we entered; the claustral, corrupt atmosphere enveloping us is the same one that once enveloped those who are speaking.

(It should be apparent only at the beginning of the following dialogue that it takes place on the radio.)

VOICE FIVE, TEXT FIVE
This should be like a drink after a celebration, back at home. Like a game: let's act like this moment is part of another story. Let's act like we're going to sleep outside, in the silence, the body

Voice six, text three (citation):
between two indistinct dates,

V5. accompanied forever

Voice six, text three (citation):
among paper flowers,

V5. by the cats.

VOICE SIX, TEXT FIVE
Everything must be done. There's no hope. The street is being watched.

V5. Let's do it right now.

V6. Are you sure this is not worse than what would happen if they found us?

V5. Yes. You won't feel a thing. Just a sudden sleep.

V6. Wouldn't it be better to open the windows, so they could come and get us? Yesterday I opened the shutters that face onto the street. It had been raining. The tram rails were glittering. A man went by on a bicycle.

Everything that had happened outside, at other times, seemed so pleasant...even visits to the dentist.

V3. Outside, on the other side of the pale, tinted panes — with their faintly colored flowers bordered by a copper frame —, the canals multiply the brick facades, the doors with their steep staircases, the white birds on the white sky. Along the banks, children were playing. Objects are reflected, surrounded with orange halos. Trees decompose on the still surface of the water — green and violet bands. We hear the bells of a church. A teenager tosses a ball

> *Voice one, text two (citation):*
> that leaves a fiery trace in the air, as if space conserved the drawing of things. The objects are formed of layers, closed with lines that continue on, beyond.

V6. Airplanes went by. We heard a bomb. Did the radio say anything?

V5. Nothing. Some classical music: still Beethoven.

V3. Along the canals, fishermen are waiting. Women are weaving, sitting under the verandas, among ceramic flowers, Indonesian screens, cages hung up on the end of poles. The children are chasing butterflies.

> *Voice three, text one (citation):*
> All of the doors and windows were open.

V3. Some children run up to our window. A few are smoking, others are holding hoops; dressed in baggy trousers. Black butterflies on their collars. Yellow faces. I can hear the street noise, and the sound they make clicking

> *Voice one, text one (citation):*
> some plastic spherules, smaller than eggs, hung at the ends of a thick string; the median point is a ring.

V3. Three little girls open their mouths — or burst out laughing? They're dressed in cobra skin and huge white hats. Their fists are closed, as if they're holding something. They raise their arms, and click their heels:

Voice one, text four (citation):
Figurines pulling strings, manikin cut-outs in the shadow-theater.

V6. What if we waited until tomorrow? (*A silence*)
Do you remember the day you dressed up as a woman? I put on your skirt and cap. (*They laugh*)

V5. Do you remember the day we had to hide? Everybody was crying. Mama opened a hat box and took out her chamberpot: «I just don't feel at home without it.» (*They laugh*)

V3. Everything is shrinking. Seems like we're suffocating. We decide that during the night, at least, we'd open up the windows. The walls were moving toward each other. The hideaway changes into a gallery with

> *Voice three, text one (citation):*
> tiny rooms crowded with old furniture...On the night-table, among flasks and spoons, a fan. Another fan on the ceiling, still, like a lamp: its black blades are covered with flies. A cradle. Pink celluloid rattles on the mosquito netting of white tulle, with silk knots.
>
> *Voice three, text five (citation):*
> An old yellow carpet, obviously home-woven, covers the floor with little flowers that must have been a bright, gaudy red.

V6. Any more water?

V5. Two glasses' worth. Let's not think about it, though. This moment is part of another story.

V6. For instance...

V5. For instance...We're at that pastry shop, the «Delphi.» No — at the «Oasis.» Do you remember?

V6. Yes, and then?

V5. Then, we meet. We're alone. It's in the afternoon. In winter. There's

American music on the record-player, and portraits of Marlene on the walls.

V6.   No. It's summer. I'm leaving school. I'm dressed in white. All neat and combed. I have a big, shiny satchel. And lipstick...How do we meet?

V5.   I come in and sit down at your table.

V6.   Without asking?

V5.   No. I say: may I sit down here? Don't you think it's hot out?

V6.   And me?

V5.   Yes.

V6.   What do we order?

V5.   Two lemonades.

V6.   The waiter who brings them is stirring them with a teaspoon.

V5.   Thank you.

V6.   You're welcome. Have some ice-cream.

(A silence.)

(CLICK-CLACK)

Voice three, text one (citation):
A gallery of tiny rooms, crowded with old furniture.

Voice three, text five (citation):
An old yellow carpet, obviously home-woven, covers the floor with little flowers that must have been a bright, gaudy red.

V4.   Outside, the rain,

V6.   the bells,

V2. a tram.

V1. At the end of the gallery,

V3. on the carpet of flowers,

V5. the body in white.

(American music from the forties)

CLIPS

SEQUENCE SIX

VOICE ONE, TEXT SIX
It was the Kumara Devi, incarnate Goddess, infant symbol of the millenary
tradition.

V3. Once the time and place of her birth had been proscribed by the
astrologers, she was searched out and installed from the first day of life,
in a palace, accompanied by a priestly retinue and her family.

V5. Made up with great care, she had to remain hidden, watched by her
matrons, never seeing the light of day. Once each year, for a few
moments, she appeared at an ornate window.

VOICE TWO, TEXT SIX
A twining screen of fornicating couples, yogi-monkeys, elephants, centaurs
with stiff white phalli and nagas served as an enormous frame for her aenemic,
waxy face, crushed by a crown.

VOICE THREE, TEXT SIX
Actually, for a few coins or a basket of fruit, tourists or the peasants who had
come down from the mountains could arrange for her to show herself, as if by
accident, forgetting her majesty during the space of a game. Her favorites —
little girls chosen to divert her — were paid accomplices; they encouraged her
to act distracted, and would even make her laugh for snapshots.

V2. At night, when the town was deserted, still being watched by her
chamber attendants, hidden behind their balconies, the Goddess would

come down onto the terrace to take the fresh air, and play, alone.

VOICE FOUR, TEXT SIX
The reign of the Kumara Devi comes to an end on the day of her first menstruation. Then, with her retinue and family, with her chaperons and servants, she leaves the palace forever.

V4. Having returned to the house where she was born, she becomes a woman like any other. The astrologers have already met to determine the time and place of her successor's birth. A cortege sets out to find her, on the day of the full moon.

> *Voice five, text six (citation):*
> The new-born is installed in the palace,
>
> *Voice six, text three (citation):*
> among paper flowers.

VOICE FIVE, TEXT SIX
In front of the temple which shelters the great drum, near the monkey-gods spotted with cinnabar, and while the pigeons on the square devour the offering-rice, the new-born is installed in the palace by the officiating priests. The cycle commences anew, a wheel that has turned for millenia, intact, like the empire, like its snowfalls and birds.

(CLICK-CLACK)

V6. There is an invisible center in every prediction: at the age of nine, while she was playing at being sick with her companions, the Kumara Devi died after drinking a sugar-water.

V2. The myth tells that she was buried in a meadow that the emperor had been excavating since the beginning of her reign: once he had gathered all of the empire into his hands, he sent thousands of laborers there.

V6. The ground was opened down to the water.

V2. Bronze was melted. A sarcophagus was brought.

V4. The palace, edifices for each of the rituals, marvellous utensils, diadems and priceless objects, all was transported and buried, the sepulchre was filled.

(The sound of rain, church bells, a tram.)

V2. The artisans were ordered to construct crossbows and bolts, so disposed that anyone who dared penetrate the tomb would pay with their life.

V4. The hundred rivers and the vast sea were fashioned with mercury.

V6. Especially constructed machines kept the silver liquid flowing, kept it passing from one groove into another.

VOICE SIX, TEXT SIX
On the vault of the tomb, all of the signs of heaven were represented; on the floor, the relief and borders of the earth. With Buffalo grease, torches were made, that would not die out soon.

V4. «May her favorites, her attendants, and her servants, may all the court follow her into death,»

V6. — ordered the emperor.

V2. When the sarcophagus had been enshrined on top of the Central Mountain — there where the square of the Earth unites with the circle of the Sky —, it was observed that the workers, the artisans who had constructed the machines and hidden the treasures, were now aware of the laws which govern the world, and might one day divulge their secret.

> *Voice five, text four (citation):*
> On the capitals, twining animals.

> *Voice six, text four (citation)*
> In the dark, the mosaics glittered on the columns.

V5. When the funerals had ended, the spiral path which led to the sepulchre was hidden, and the outer door closed again.

> *Voice six, text six (citation):*
> On the vault of the tomb, all of the signs of heaven were represented; on the floor, the relief and borders of the earth. With Buffalo grease, torches were made, that would not die out soon.

V4. Darkness fell.

V2. The funereal jewels, which had lost their glittering angles, grew faint and gray, moonlike.

V4. On a background of grey moss, diadems: untouched ruins.

V6. All those who had constructed and hidden the treasures, workers and artisans, remained there, enclosed forever.

V2. Men standing still.

V3. Mute,

V5. changed into wooden toys.

V6. And then their bones covered the floor of the underground gallery, in a spiral ending at the coffin where the Goddess lay, two spheres of jade clasped in her hands.

V2. A bed of still flowers,

V4. a garden of white angles:

V6. the motionless river of vertebrae traced circles around the central mountain, whence arose the resinous odor of balm.

V3. On the tomb, herbs and bushes were planted.

V5. The tomb became a meadow again.

V4. Below, the gallery was sinking,

V6. sown with bones,

V2. still white flowers.

V1. And at the highest point of this doubling world,

V3. on the carpet of flowers,

V5. as if alive, the body in white.

(Nepalese ritual music)

CLIPS

RE-CITE
combine-hearing

«I call what I make 'combine-paintings,' that is combined works, combinations. I want to avoid categories this way. If I had called what I make paintings, people would have told me they were sculptures, and if I had called them sculptures then people would have told me they were paintings.»

«A pair of shoes is just as useful in making a painting as wood, nails, turpentine, oil paint, canvas...»

Robert Rauschenberg

«There is no more of a subject in a 'combine-painting' than in a newspaper page: everything there is a subject.»

John Cage

CHARACTERS

Five young male voices:
cobra: COB
tundra: TUN
scorpion: SCO
totem: TOT
tiger: TIG

a bartender, same as the monk: BAR
a monk, same as the bartender: MON
a speaker: SPE
an assistant: ASS
a little blond junky from the rembrandtplein: BLO

MUSIC

A musical anthology of the Orient. Tibet II.
Unesco, BM 30 L 2010

Dionne Warwick.
Vogue Records, ELP 8 168

With the participation of:

the classified page of the *Justice Weekly*
*
the scientific page of the daily *Le Monde*
*
the text of Lichtenstein's canvas *Hopeless,* 1963
*
a page from William Seward Burroughs' *Naked Lunch*
*

a description by Giancarlo Marmori, in *Ceremony of a Body*
*
a description by Chen fou, in *Tales of a Floating Life*
*
several passages from *Cobra*

NOTE: Speeches placed beneath one another and italicized should be spoken simultaneously.

The version of *Re-cite* translated here contains additional material (the Rembrandtplein bar scene) that was not included in the version published in *Para la voz*.

Tibetan music

COB. Plexiglass flowers opening. The same record starts again, in English. *Where were we?* Vinyl circles,

TUN. *Where were we?*

SCO. *Where were we?*

TOT. *Where were we?*

TIG. *Where were we?*   turning, overlapping. Hum of Japanese cameras. Doubled images. Reflected symmetry. Multiplied. A succession of overexposed photographs...On the whiteness of a magazine cover. *Looking for what?*

TUN.   *Looking for what?*

SCO.   *Looking for what?*

TOT.   *Looking for what?*

TIG.   *Looking for what?* A porcelain head inscribed with black ideograms. Intersection of edges. Volumes of bakelite. *Everything is happening in the present.* Empty sequences. A rendez-

TUN. *Everything is happening in the present.*

SCO. *Everything is happening in the present.*

TOT. *Everything is happening in the present.*

COB. *Everything is happening in the present.*

TIG. *Everything is happening in the present.* vous. Who was waiting for me? A small wooden door — I passed through it almost without noticing. Then I was heading down a corridor, over a black carpet, a rhythmic pattern of tigers and white letters. I could hear my breathing, my footsteps. I felt the sole of my foot settle into the carpet and rise again, heel first. Almost without noticing, I was heading down a corridor. At the end, on the wall, black on white, a drawing. *Two men fighting.*

COB.   *Or maybe not.*

TIG.   ...Or maybe not: white on black, two men, the same, leaping *toward each other,* embracing. Unarmed. Naked.

SCO.   *Or maybe not.*

TOT.   *Other silhouettes.* The scene was projected onto the wall; *the two possible scenes.*

TIG.   *Or maybe not.*

TOT.   *Other silhouettes.*

SCO.   *The same men.* It was there, in front of the projector, that the four of them appeared. In front of the projector. *Where were we?*

TIG.   *Where were we?*

TOT.   *Where were we?*

SCO.   *Where were we?*

TUN.   *Where were we?*
         You were right to come. Enter.

COB.   Showing me to the bar.

TUN.   Today's your day.

COB.   Boots, of course, a jacket and cracked leather belt: and everything in black. His straight hair fell to his shoulders in greasy tangles.

TUN.   We've been waiting.

(Cobra and Scorpion reading simultaneously)

COB. Around his neck, at the end of a chain with thick, forged links, a tin rosette. On the back of his jacket, tattoed into the leather, his name: «Tundra». In shining black on the dull black of the hide.

SCO. Los Angeles, Calif., USA: Good-looking man of 33, height 5'10'' (photo and particulars available) interested in meeting a good-looking, well-built, education-minded dominant male, possibly motorcycle-type leather fan.

COB. *His thick wrists*

TOT. *His thick wrists.*

COB. *Tattoed with eagles.*

TIG. *Tattoed with eagles.*

COB. *Surrounded with bracelets.*

TOT. *Surrounded with bracelets.*

COB. *His cracked boots.*

TIG. *His thick wrists.*

COB. *His cracked boots.*

TOT. *Surrounded with bracelets.*

(Cobra and Scorpion as before)

COB. Around his neck, at the end of a chain with thick, forged links, a tin rosette. On the back of his jacket, tattoed into the leather, his name: «Tundra». In shining black on the dull black of the hide.

91

SCO. New York, N.Y., USA: Handsome male of 30, of docile nature, well-built, wishes to meet or correspond with boot-wearing men interested in the subject of discipline.

(Tibetan music)

TOT. We had entered the bar. The entire length of one wall was taken up by an aquarium. On the inside; little neon lamps, submerged among the stones and white polystrene coral, under motionless, fluorescent glass seahorses and lily-white rustproof flowers in full bloom. A clear light was emanating from the botton, filtered by the algae, lighting the shelves filled with bottles, the screens, the Turkish stools. A whiteness crossed by slow shadows, with fins vibrating like black butterflies. Tundra was dancing. Another one of them came up next to me. His name was carved into his jacket, among the chairs and medaillons: «Scorpion». He handed me something to drink, his eyes bloodshot. He was laughing.

SCO. Look!

(He laughs)

Behind the counter, three nude women, of gold!

COB. Pressed against his neck, a funeral amulet. In the center, protected by two pieces of cut glass, surrounded by amber beads, a pile of small, porous bones with sharp edges: baby teeth and bird cartilage. It was knotted in a thin ribbon of white silk, faded, with gothic initials

TUN. *with gothic initials*

TOT. *and German names*

COB.   and German names, traced in black ink.
     I remember.

TIG. *In black ink.*

TUN. *I remember.*

TOT.   *I remember.*

TIG.   *I remember.*

                (an old door opens. boys' laughter, mocking,
                erotic, vague.
                through an echo chamber.)

COB.   I remember. The amulet. What was it he made me drink? A buzzing in my ears. A metallic taste in my mouth. Colors bursting. Things surrounded with halos: blue, violet, orange, white. A silence. Time receding. Something motionless, striking me. *Galaxy in white.* A sign

TOT.   *Galaxy in white.*
      splitting. *Green.* Less green. White. A snake *coiling.* And

TIG.   *White.*   *White.*

TUN.   glistening. *Gleaming scales.* White. More green. *Green.* A splitting

TIG.   *Splitting signs.*

SCO.   *White.*

      sign. *Galaxy in white.*

TOT.   *Galaxy in white.*

TIG.   *Galaxy in white.*

COB.   How much time had gone by? Behind the aquarium, as if someone had drawn back a curtain, a stretch of sand appeared. On the sand, zebras were fleeing in all directions. Slowly. Heading farther away, drawing closer again. A checkerboard landscape. Parallel bands spreading behind the glass. Long necks twining; tails and manes waving in slow motion. Lips pressed to the glass, slobbering strings of drool.

                (a torrent)

The zebras were leaping in rows, at regular intervals. A row of black zebras striped white. They rose up, behind the aquarium, hovering,

falling back down, front legs tucked under, then rose again, fleeing in disorder...while another row took their place. The lights behind the bar went out.
Bit by bit, a small stage was illuminated by the relectors.

> (from the café-theater stage, with echo, comes the voice of)

TUN. The American astronomer Allan Robert Sandage, at the astrophysical congress currently being held in Texas, revealed that in June 1966 astronomers at the Mount Palomar Observatory witnessed one of the largest explosions of a celestial object ever witnessed by man.

The astronomical object in question is a qusar bearing the number 3-C-466. Quasars, first discovered in 1963, are young, extremely distant (several light billion years away) and luminous stars. The explosion they observed, which multiplied the surface brightness of quasar 3-C-466 twentyfold within the space of a few weeks, was thus produced billions of years ago, probably shortly after the initial explosion which, according to Professor Sandage's theory, gave birth to the universe as we know it today.

> (small cascade)

COB. Backdrop: bleeding skeletons cling to the caryatids of a white mausoleum. In a corner, a blond teenager with shining feet, biting a pear and painting his skin. Over his heart, a heart; then yellow circles surrounding red rings, which surround black rings; and above, arrows and ciphers. He encloses all this in a cloud of white brushstrokes. Applause. The lights went down.

> (from the café-theater stage, with echo, the officially erotic, light, relaxing voice of an airline stewardess)

ASS. And now, ladies and gentlemen, the final report from the National Electronics Conference in Chicago...

> (applause)

SPE. (in a flat shopgirl voice)
I want to sound a word of warning. The logical extension of

encephalographic research is biocontrol, that is control of physical movement, mental processes, emotional reactions and *apparent* sensory impressions by means of bioelectric signals injected into the nervous system of the subject...Shortly after birth, a surgeon could install connections in the brain. A miniature radio receiver could be plugged in and the subject controlled from the SS, that is the STATE-CONTROLLED SENDERS.

ASS.   The biocontrol apparatus is a prototype of one-way telepathic control. The subject could be rendered susceptible to the transmitter by drugs or other processes without installing any apparatus. Ultimately the senders will use telepathic transmitting exclusively... Do you know the principle behind the Mayan codices?

SPE.   The priests — about one percent of the population — devised a system of one-way telepathic broadcasts instructing the workers what to feel and when. The telepathic Sender had to send twenty-four hours out of twenty-four.

> (hurrahs, applause. In the distance, the sound
> of guitars in cheap cafés)

COB.   New backdrop: along the banks of a still, white river, flaming pyres of bluish corpses, with sulfurized feet and eyes covered with mushrooms. Behind, in the night, more pyres. Projected onto a tulle veil, black and yellow dots are forming a face: a sobbing blond. Enormous tears. Gushing from her lips, in a balloon, this inscription: «That's the way it *should* have begun! But it's hopeless!» Silence. The lights went down.

> (applause. The speaker's voice begins again,
> with an echo from the little stage)

SPE.   Man, my dear colleagues, as I was saying, thanks to the Sender, cannot receive anything by himself, because that would mean that someone else besides the Sender has feelings of his own, which could louse up the Sender's continuity. So the Sender has to send all the time, but he can't ever recharge himself by contact. And the result is that sooner or later he's got no feelings to send...

ASS.   Finally, the screen would go dead, and the Sender was transformed into a huge black centipede...So the workers came in on the beam, burned the centipede and elected a new Sender by consensus of the general will.

SPE.   The Mayans were limited by isolation. But now, one Sender could control the planet...I want to emphasize once more that control is not and can never be a «means» to any practical «end»...It can never be a means to anything but more control and more slavery...

> (the assistant interrupts and they pronounce the next phrase together)

SPE and ASS.   Like junk.

> (applause. cheering)

SPE and ASS.   Thank you, thank you.

> (applause. cheering)

COB.   It was then that one of the boys, the one with the name «Tiger» on his jacket, started banging on the aquarium with the palms of his hands. Slow, flat animals approached: lanceolated, spreading, symmetrical leaves with tenuous nerves. Streaked with mercury. Mayan faces. Their orange flagella followed, winding around them, incandescent.

BAR.   Will you stop banging on that glass!

COB.   Like a jack-in-the-box, the bartender appeared in a doorway.

BAR.   Get out of here, you hoodlums!

TIG.   What's your problem? You don't like it? You want me to pronounce one word, one single syllable, and turn you into a bird? You want me to conjure up five thousand minor demons right this minute, to prick you, to poison your precious bodily fluids? Make me a gin and tonic instead.

> (Tibetan music)

COB.   We left. *Everything had changed.*

TUN.   *Everything had changed*

COB.   *After how long? For which return?*

SCO.   *After how long?*

TOT.   *For which return?*

COB.   *The corridor was white.* On the floor, arranged in an indecipherable

TUN.   *The corridor was white.*

SCO.   *The corridor was white.*

TOT.   *The corridor was white.*

TIG.   *The corridor was white.*
sequence, there were cubes of tinted plastic and red metal bands that curved back on themselves, forming rings.

TOT.   The door facing the street opened automatically. We could hardly stand the glare from the shop windows. Bar noises were echoing in our ears. It was raining. From the square, we could hear guitars in the cafés, far away. A frightened woman appeared by the subway entrance, very pale. She was wearing a wide brimmed red hat, with ribbons that fell onto her black cape, hiding the gold flowers on her face.

SCO.   She wore screaming make-up, and her mouth was painted in a floral pattern. Her eye sockets were black, with silver shadow, joined beneath the eyebrows, then extended in volutes of rouge and powdered metal as far as the temples and down to the nostrils; wide, arabesque outlines, like swans' eyes, but of richer, more varied colors. Instead of lashes, a fringe of tiny jewels dangled from her eyelids. She was a woman from the neck down, but above the body blossomed into a kind of baroque-snouted heraldic beast.

COB.   We crossed the city. We were in the suburbs; the landscape had changed. *The landscape had changed.* Pines,

TOT.   *The landscape had changed.*   cypresses and plum-trees appeared through the mist. We were following a narrow gorge.

97

One of the walls fell off vertically, carved sheer, like a screen; different veins of sand crossed, a play of motionless waves, so smooth and polished we could see our reflections. Our voices and the sound of our feet padding through the wet grass rang back off the walls of the stone corridor, but opaque and deformed, distant, from our *former lives.* The other slope was less

TUN.   *former lives.*

SCO.   *former lives.*

TOT.   *former lives.*

TIG.   *former lives.*   steep; wild olive trees grew from the crevices, branches were hanging down the walls, among blossoming tree peonies, ferns, lianas. Dwarf fig trees had sprouted up between the rocks.

(guitars in the distance)

SCO.   On the ridge, frost covered a thicket of willows, whose branches blended into the frozen streams, falling in a casade of filaments. Behind the graygreen rapids, touches of white, acacia branches; swollen, milky stalks, pistils oozing resin, mauve stipules with watery lumps articulated like cartilage, trembling corrollas whose filaments snapped shut as we passed. There were cranes nesting in the colorless rushes, dry as match-sticks. Beating wings and wild birds' cries announced our approach. As we climbed, the sound of the water grew louder.

(sound of a street in a modern city)

TOT.   Ropes hung from the highest clefts, flush to the rock, with baskets slung onto the ends. In some of the crevices, marked out by wattle screens on the rock face, monks lived alone, naked, mute examiners of the void.

TIG.   The birds knew them and nested close by: fluttering and chirping round the hampers, where pilgrims left tea and barley meal, they guided these rare devotees to the foot of the anchorites' refuge.

COB.   *Around a bend in the wall,* some young peasants appeared.

TUN. *They laughed when they noticed us.*

COB. *They were searching for mushrooms.*

SCO. *So many foreigners around here.*

(Dionne Warwick)

COB. They laughed when they noticed us, as if surprised to see so many foreigners around. They followed us. For a long time, we could hear their vague, mocking laughter echoing after us. They left us near a frozen stream, where the hermits cross on a blue buffalo when they retire from the world.

TUN. Following the widening meanders, which were bordered by polished stones, angular like the vertebrae of giant reptiles, we reached a narrow grotto whre the stream ended in a limpid pool. A dark red grass was growing on the white sand at the bottom.

(Tibetan music)

COB. There, beneath the great foot, en su salsa, the faithful are seated. A strong urine stench, among other smells — there's a poster for «The Wild One» and the bubble coming out of its mouth says «MEN» — cuts through an odor of hash and, get a good deep whiff now, the stink of a filthy dive in the Malay Archilepago; none of which bothers any of them. A green neon tube curves to form the heel, traces the toes sinuously, and the arch with a straight line. The darkened sole is in chalk.

Through shifting layers of uselessly mentholated smoke, you can see the babyfoot players, glued to the handles; behind, a naked man lashed to a stake — the door to the «WOMEN». On the walls, giant photos of girls in transparent kimonos, racing cars, a Nepalese temple, Karen Appel, Che Guevara. Flowers. In between two records — endlessly repeated — you hear pinball machines, clicking flippers, fists pounding the wood; lights flicker on the backboards, dropping strawberries, clubs, lemons, cherries. Without a photoelectric cell, without anybody pushing it, the big, cracked door onto the Rembrandtplein swings back, slow and ponderous: the guru has arrived.

GUR. My head...

COB. He says, adding another gesture to the five ritual thingies that signaled his entrance, while the players continue to mill around the machines...

GUR. My head has the perfection of an egg, my eyes that of lotus petals, my lips the fullness of the mango. The arch of my eyebrows alludes to the Krishna. Fix me a tableful of rice. And, I beg you *please,* keep your hands off me...

COB. He dismisses the curious with a hand reeking of incense; he shoves his clients away...

GUR. Ask your questions from afar. Every man for himself. Humanity? I could care less. And quit that sighing. I travel by jet, not elephant. Holiness? Screw it.

COB. And then the Most High One takes off his orange hat, and the rings — fake tiger teeth — he wears on each finger. He drops onto a bench, beneath the great neon foot, among torn cushions, knapsacks, shoes. In the dust cloud that rises, some startled hippies mumble, shove him over, turn around, and go back to sleep. The Master pulls off his shoes — sandals despite the cold —, scattering glass beads and brass rings. He selects one of his Indian scarves for the night, and one of his blondest followers for a lover. Hand in hand they cross the smoke-filled room, through the rows of players and the gaping door of the «MENS». The mustard light reveals a graffitied wall and two urinals clogged with thick, opalescent water. The guru caresses the blond's forehead:

GUR. You have been chosen from all the rest...

COB. He reams him softly. And the little blond comes in a flash...

BLO. O! — Isles of the Blessed!

COB. And grabs hold of a faucet.

BLO. I can see the Western Heavens...

COB. In front of a dulled mirror, the Supreme One shoots up. He emerges from the john most cryptic.

GUR. What a stench of burning grass! Verily verily I say unto thee, any damn thing is the truth. A true god is indistinguishable from a fool or a clown. More ice, please. Barbarism, thy name is the Western World.

(Dionne Warwick)

COB. Behind us, the grotto opened onto a misty landscape, successive planes evaporating into white toward the horizon, where a layer of moisture floated over a lake. We could make out tree trunks, bent by the wind, long silvery leaves, broken in the middle, hanging down.

TOT. Farther on, a barge and a small landing. In the dew, we could see *a bamboo forest, white on white.*

TUN. *white on white*

COB. *a bamboo forest.*

TOT. And rising above,

SCO. the towers of a monastery. As we penetrated the fog, forms appeared, *colors emerged.*

TIG. *White on white.*

COB. Pheasants were flying from branch to branch in front of us, never far, unable to balance, burdened with ornaments, heavy, slow in the viscous air. We heard a noise in the rushes. *It was a tiger fleeing.*

TUN. *Covered with black signets.*

COB. *It was a tiger fleeing.*

SCO. *It was a tiger fleeing.*

TOT. Striped with orange.

TIG. A tiger of painted paper.

COB. *Striped with orange.*

TOT.   *Of painted paper.*

COB.   Clearing a path through the dense stalks that surrounded us, skirting
       the lake in the direction of the towers, we came to the foot of a stone
       wall, crumbling from the pressure of thorn-bushes growing in its
       joints and fissures. We followed it until we found an opening: a road
       wound upward on the other side, over an arched bridge, leading to
       the monastery gate, which was crowned by a black lacquered plaque
       bearing the inscription:

                            Top of the Pops,

                            (Tibetan music)
                            (bar noises)

       almost erased. The guru was there, surrounded by his fans...

SCO.   What must I do to be freed from the reincarnation cycle?

GUR.   Learn to breathe.

                    (applause. laughter. silence.)

COB.   An Abyssinian athelete faints. Slippping through an open window,
       forefingers on their lips, four nude pin-up girls: when they reach the
       center of the room they pull four Salvation Army uniforms and four
       giant donation boxes out of their bags. They face the four cardinal
       points and start soliciting. Fracas of florins.

TOT.   How does one speak to God?

GUR.   Seated. Left foot on the right thigh, right foot on the left thigh.
       Cross your arms behind your back. Hold your left heel with your
       right hand, right heel with the left. Lower your head, chin on the
       chest. Concentrate on your navel.
           And then...try to get out of it...

                    (laughter. sighs. silence.)

COB.   A little Morrocan with grape-colored pupils is dancing: a Dutchman
       sprinkles his head, an astrakhan carpet, with brown beer that runs

down his back, between his cheeks. Don Luis de Góngora y Argote emerges from a gumball machine.

TIG.   What's the quickest way to achieve liberation?

GUR.   Not to think about it.

                    (sighs. shouts of approval.)

COB.   Shirley Temple pops out of the «MEN». A spade is unscrewing the backboard of a pinball machine: he hides a kif ball in each light-bulb and a syringe in the aluminum ball-loader.

TUN.   What formula must I repeat so as not to be reincarnated as a pig?

GUR.   Ubiquitous is the whiteness of celestial purity and happiness; ubiquitous the snowy, shadowless, immutable bodies of the divine.

        Marine, invisible, ever blue, the demi-gods and weightless ones surround us.

        Neither word nor object, in his yellow world of successive circles, man is in motion.

        No joy is mine. Beneath my feet hide antelopes of grass, birds and serpents of mint.

        Have you listened to the racket of the gnomes, their fuss against the red walls?

        O Humanity, what demons, what blackness befalls you, like night descending upon the plain.

               (finger cymbals, a bone flute)

Religion, my dears, is merely sound.

                      (sighs)

Qué vida la mia! I travel east for the spring equinox, south for the summer solstice, to the heart of the darkest West at the onset of autumn, and to the far north in the dead of winter. Goodbye, goodbye...

COB.   As he goes out the door, the Unique One turns once more to the distracted crowd, and concludes:

GUR.   Eat your flowers...

(Dionne Warwick)

COB.   As the door was opened, the face of Buddha appeared before our eyes. His gold colors combined their reflections with those of the green fronds which shaded him, and covered a stone staircase and the base of the pillars. Continuing to the west and then turning northward, we ascended through a slanting gallery leading directly to the reception hall, which consisted of three trussed bays. The room faced directly onto the great rock, over twenty feet high, in the shape of the «man-t'eou» — like a sugarloaf. A thin ring of bamboo adorned the base. At the foot of the rock was a fountain in the shape of a crescent moon, fed by spring water and covered with thick tufts of a kind of watercress. The sanctuary proper was to the east of the reception hall.

TUN.   It was dark, in ruins, and invaded by the damp from all sides. On the floor, there was a dark green crust which thickened in spots, forming yellowish, granular lumps with white edges. A grey lichen covered the three stone walls; tiny purple flowers were spreading outward from the corners from the goiters of black, leprous pulp.

SCO.   Signs of rust striped the vaulting: they almost seemed traced in saffron. Perspiration drops formed, and lingered for a long moment in suspense, before dripping onto the mold with a crisp smack.

COB.   The great Buddha and the ruins of an altar lay at the end of the room, in front of a window where large, roughly cut, curving leaves filtered out the bright light.

TIG.   On the bas-relief decorating the plinth, a god danced in a fiery hoop, trampling a dwarfish devil; a cobra coiled around one of his right arms and the hand shook a tambourine, while a flame rose from one of the hands on the left.

COB.   In the circle of fire, a nest *of mushrooms.*

TIG.   *of molluscs.*

TUN.   On the god's crown, mushrooms were growing.

104

TIG.   *Mushrooms were growing* on the god's crown.

TOT.   *A nest of molluscs.*

SCO.   *Molluscs were growing.*

COB.   Behind the window, hidden by the leaf-work, were twisting roots, swollen and white, with glossy, bone-like nodes covered by wine-colored veins. Black rootlets were hanging from the fern branches into the sun, intercepting the light.
       On the roots. Like a mane. Into the pond.

TUN.   *On the roots.*

TOT.   *Like a mane.*

TIG.   *Into the pond.*

SCO.   Into the pond, like a mane, on the roots, hanging, *in the light,* from the fern branches,

COB.   *black fibers*

SCO.   *Black fibers.*

TIG.   *Veiling the light.*

TOT.   *Like a mane.*

TUN.   *Into the pond.*

COB.   The floor was so slippery we could hardly walk. Joining hands, we managed to get as far as the pond. The water was cloudy; in the shadow of roots split by the refraction, misshapen yet symmetrical ivories, slow, bloated fish, bulbous like the roots, drifted in vegetal sumber, wrapped in jelly-like veils and a bush of fibers and flagella.

TIG.   Letting us touch them.

TOT.   Not fleeing.

TUN.   Among the roots.

SCO.   Misshapen ivories.

COB.   Slumbering.

TUN.   Bloated.

SCO.   Slow.

TOT.   Letting us touch them. *Not fleeing.*

TIG.   *Not fleeing.*

COB.   *Slumbering. Bloated. Slow.*

TUN.   *Slumbering.*

SCO.   *Bloated.*

TOT.   *Slow.*

COB.   We were mistaken: there was no window, no open gap in the mountain-side. Spreading back the huge leaves, we could see leeches clinging to the thin transparent blades, no doubt doubled; beads of water lay still, like mercury in a spirit level. Some light reached us through the foliage, and we could vaguely make out the sandy mass of the rock, far away, on the other side. *A greenhouse light.*

TUN.   *A greenhouse light.*

SCO.   *A greenhouse light.*

TIG.   *A greenhouse light.*

COB.   We were about to leave when Tiger slipped and fell headlong into the pond.

TIG.   I banged on the aquarium with the palms of my hands.

COB.   Slow, flat animals approached: lanceolated, spreading, symmetrical leaves with tenuous nerves. Streaked with mercury. Mayan faces. Their orange flagella followed, winding around them, incandescent. On the other side of the glass, *slow, flat animals, lanceolated...*

TUN.   *slow, flat animals,*

SCO.   *lanceolated...*

COB.   *Spreading, symmetrical leaves,*

TOT.   *Spreading, symmetrical leaves,*

COB.   *with tenuous nerves.*

TIG.   *with tenuous nerves.*

COB.   *Streaked with mercury. Mayan faces.*

TUN.   *Streaked with mercury.*

SCO.   *Mayan faces.*

TOT.   *Mayan faces.*

TIG.   *Streaked with mercury.*

COB.   We helped him up. The fish had scattered everywhere. Then, like a
        jack-in-the-box, a monk of the red hat sect appeared in a doorway:

MON.   You want me to say one word, one single syllable, and turn you into
        a bird? You want me to conjure up five thousand minor demons
        right this minute, to prick you, to poison your precious bodily
        fluids?
                Get out of here, you hoodlum!

                        (silence)

COB.   We left. *Everything had changed.*

TUN.   *Everything had changed.*

SCO.   *Everything had changed.*

TOT.   *Everything had changed.*

TIG.   *Everything had changed.*

107

COB.   I wrap around myself, elbows against my stomach.

TUN.   The room is white.

SCO.   Black objects flee toward the walls, ex-orbited: centrifugal force.

TOT.   The floor is tilting. The walls dilate.

TIG.   Falling, immobile, the body.

COB.   Petals, filaments.

TUN.   (Left foot over my right thigh.)

COB.   The body is inscribed in a net.

SCO.   (Right foot over left thigh.)

COB.   Six flowers mark the median line.

TOT.   (I cross my arms behind my back.)

COB.   Tendrils, branching from flowers, in all directions, forking, twining.

TIG.   (I grasp my left heel with my right hand; right heel with the left.)

COB.   Man is opaque; the golden skein.

TUN.   (I lower my head, chin on chest)

SCO.   A somber halo, a *continuous, black* line bounds his figure,

COB.   *black,*   *continuous*

TOT.   crossed by glowing traces.

TIG.   Each of his gestures, even the most *sudden, or slight,* echoes

COB.   *slight, or sudden*
         throughout his frame, like a fright through the fins

TUN.   *throughout his frame,*

SCO.   *throughout his frame,*

TOT.   *throughout his frame,*

TIG.   *throughout his frame,*

COB.   of a fish. *White.*

TUN.   *White.*

SCO.   *White.*

TOT.   *White.*

TIG.   *White.*

THE ANT-KILLERS

Note

The Ant-killers is a text on decolonization: of territories and of bodies. Of territories: Portugal restores liberty to its colonies. The play attempts to take political discourse into account according to a «different» method; it appears here as neither a program nor a scrupulous *engagement*, but as a marginal element — political events reach us only through the mediation of radio newscasts — which gradually takes on body and inserts itself among other bodies, pushing them, in turn, into the margin. And likewise for the world of sound; the basic elements — borrowed from the music of the former Portugese colonies — progressively accept others which dismantle them, pushing them toward the edge of the page, and of our hearing.

Decolonization of the body: liberated sexuality, liberation of the voice. What one character says, in the last analysis, could just as well be said by another. By this means we attempt a destruction of radiophonic dialogue, an archaic form of communication between two voices in which one is always trying to «colonize» the other. We want to set a pulverised narrative into motion here, a galaxy of voices at the heart of which individualities and verbal tenses contradict and annual themselves.

Destruction of the individual as destruction of another metropolis — the conscience or the soul — reigning over its colonies — the voice, sex, etc.

Dissolution of the self.

Voices

Six French tourists in Portugal: four men — M1, M2, M3, M4 — and two women — W1, W2.
Two other tourists: the voices M1 and M2 in sequence II, and M3 and M4 in sequence III.
Four French photographers in Angola: M1, M2 and W1, W2.
Two Portugese soldiers: either the voices M3 and M4, or two other voices.

Sound Elements

The sound elements should be joined very simply, with no transition whatsoever, as in a cut-up. The elements are as follows:

1. Music from Guinea Bissau.
2. Music from Mozambique.
3. A car braking.
4. Music from Angola.
5. A public meeting or demonstration.
6. Michel Delpech's song, *Ça ira.*
7. Traditional Brazilian music.
8. Music from Goa.
9. African birds.
10. Portuguese music.
11. *Lady in Satin,* by Billy Holliday.
12. The first sentence of this play.

The elements are delivered in the following order:
1 - 2
1 - 3 - 2
1 - 3 - 4 - 2
1 - 3 - 5 - 4 - 2
1 - 3 - 5 - 6 - 4 - 2
7 - 8
7 - 9 - 8
7 - 9 - 10 - 8
7 - 9 - 11 - 10 - 8
7 - 9 - 11 - 12 - 10 - 8
7 - 9 - 11 - 12 - 10 - 8

SEQUENCE I

M1. This takes place in Portugal. And the first thing you hear, in the distance, is the sound of brakes. Or rather: the screech of tires skidding on a road, like a car side-slipping, full speed, around a bend.

M2. Then a few seconds of silence. Not even the wind. Nor the leaves of the olive trees. Nor the sea. A few seconds of silence. And the crash; pulverised glass scattering. Smashed, trampled. Bursting in splinters.

M3. Then a silence again. But very different from the first. Peopled, as if behind a white wall, or with various sounds, like shapes under water. Sounds extinguished, effaced, erased by the wind: a woman's voice, other voices. The sound of another car's brakes. A radio. A bird.

M4. So this takes place in Portugal, on a solid blue background, bright, acrylic. Overexposed, pasted, cut-up, with a close-up's clarity, a striped, colored fabric is unfolding slowly, opening like a flower, in slow motion. Plain geometries, blood red, chlorophyll green. Plain: like paper cut up by children, or the Chinese game of striped triangles — cock, house and boat. An opening shirt. Peeled off, slowly, by the sleeves. Unbuttoned. And then

M1. held

M2. open,

M3. hurting the eyes.

M4. Horizontal stripes. A square. With a bar across the top.

M1. A striped shirt that a boy unfurls, bare-chested, at the top of a hill. Unbuttoned. Not to take it off, or to put it on, but to make signals visible from a distance: as if with a flag.

M2. Gleaming with oil, muscled, barechested. Barefoot. His bare feet on the burning sand. Big teeth. Clear eyes. Canvas trousers with a studded leather belt. A bulging crotch, like a negro's, or on the cover of a gay magazine in Amsterdam.

Sound elements (very short)
1 - 2

W1. Just like all French leftists, we changed our vacation plans when we heard the first reports of the April Revolution in Portugal, and decided to go and see the new regime, as if it were a matter of a three-star hotel, or something really quaint. We wanted to photograph everything in a few days. We had just spent the afternoon in a little fishing port near Faro, buying porcelain plates to go with blue that would pile up in the attic, embroidered napkins that would yellow in the cabinet.

W2. On a large square of beaten earth, near the sea, under a tent, deserted bump-cars spun and collided, empty. In the village, the wind stirred up clouds of dust, gusting, carrying the loudspeakers' tinny music, as if close by, but then barely audible; and the odor of grilled sardines from a bar with low windows, where blacks from the port piled in to drink beer all afternoon.

W1. It was a French song, full of clever allusions to the revolution.

M1. (*humming*) — Ah, que Marianne était jolie quand elle chantait sur les toits, ça ira, ça ira.

W1. The coast wind was blowing through the village, carrying the crashing of the brightly colored aluminum cars, under the deserted tent,

M1. the sardine smell and the smoke,

M2. the whining voice on the record,

M3. sand,

M4. dust.

117

W1. We had left the village at dusk. We wanted to make up for lost time. We were driving full speed along the coast road.

M1. The bright colors of a signal distracted me.

M2. Blood red, green,

M3. a naked boy was opening and closing a striped shirt.

M4. Alone,

M1. at the top of a hill.

W1. Not noticing, we were driving very fast.

M2. The tires screeched.

M3. The broken glass.

M4. The car radio was still on.

Sound elements
1 - 3 - 2

(On the car radio, the end of a newcast; three chimes, the beginning of a fourth.)

M1. (*as a radio announcer*) ...where he will undertake negotiations with members of the British government.

(Three chimes)

M2. (*same*) Nearly twenty thousand today participated in a demonstration to express their joy at the announcement of the end of the colonial wars, and acclaimed the promise of liberation announced to the peoples of Angola, Guinea and Mozambique. A crowd gathered in front of the Belem palace to express their solidarity with the historic speech delivered on Saturday by the President of the Republic.

(The news which follows is heard in the background; in the foreground, the sound of an approaching car, more brakes, voices, etc.)

M3. (*still as announcer*) With Portugal's sincere gesture, a new era is beginning for Africa, declared the President of the O.A.U. The acting President of the O.A.U., Somalian chief of state General Mohamed Siad Barré, happily received the announcement delivered on Saturday by the President concerning the movement of the Portugese armed forces, affirming the Capital's recognition of its African territories' right to independence...

Sound elements
1 - 3 - 4 - 2

SEQUENCE II

M1. At the top of the hill, the ant-killers were camping.

M2. We were following a narrow, sandy trail, dotted with underbrush, which left the coast to cross the road, and then the tracks of a little yellow train that looked like a toy; winding through the dunes, it disappeared into the maquis.

M1. From the dune, near a tent, a boy was watching us. His trousers were cut from the same canvas, from the same blue.

M2. He was big. He was smiling at us. Long hair, ruffled, blond, burnt. A red strip around his neck. A scarf, perhaps.

M1. No: an African choker, with several rows of stones, forming symmetries; animals' silhouettes cut down the middle, sliced in two.

M2. We drew closer. He had clear eyes; very big teeth. More red stones around his wrist. An absent gaze.

M1. With the rudiments of several languages, we struck up a banal conversation. He was living in this tent with two friends who were roaming in the maquis right now, with nothing for funiture but a transistor, a primo stove and three blankets. They were students, and occasionally jazz musicians. They wanted to visit Amsterdam, to buy some grass. They knew *Lady in Satin* by heart and sang it with exaggerated *ch*s.

M2. They were observing a continuous fiesta, broken by alimentary intermissions. Besides their tent, they had brought along their bathing suits and habitual boredom. For the moment, their sole occupation consisted of exterminating the ants which were ruthlessly beseiging the ephemeral provisions they possessed: a few packets of soup, an opened can of sardines, and a pound of sugar.

M1. They had organized their defense in concentric circles. An outer circle, or no-man's land, where enemy movements were tolerated, but closely observed as an alert was sounded. An intermediate circle, where extermination was attempted with a bombardment of stones. An inner circle, where they resorted to heavy manoeuvres: sand and fire.

M2. They had perfected brutal methods of genocide: they flooded the colonies with salt water and burned them, pursuing the survivors, pounding them with pine branches, back to their holes. They'd even squandered their last *escudos* on an insect bomb.

M1. On the pretext of showing us the destruction from the last preventive reaction strike, he led us back to the tent.

M2. A sweltering heat and a bluish, dense light, filtered by the canvas, filled the inside.

M1. Carefully, he picked up the stove and a jar of water, then set them down outside. He didn't see any reason why all three of us shouldn't make love.

M2. He went back outside the tent, still naked, shirt in hand. From the inside, we saw him open and close it, arms raised, as if to signal in the direction of the underbrush.

M1. The others, perhaps, saw it. They were waiting, perhaps, for the agreed signal to come back.

M2. We heard the whistle of the narrow-guage train, shrill and hesitant, like that of a toy; and saw, very distinctly, spurts of vapor rising in rings from the locomotive's smokestack.

M1. A child's drawing: the train, the steam, the black wheels, the yellow cars, the sun.

M2. We heard the train heading away.

M1. And then,

M2. a car's brakes.

M1. No: screeching tires.

M2. A brief silence.

M1. Broken glass.

M2. Scattered.

M1. Silence again.

M2. The train, very far away. A woman's voice. The wind. A song, on the radio, in French. (He hums the song *Ça ira*)

Sound elements
1 - 3 - 5 - 4 - 2

SEQUENCE III

M2. We continued in the direction of the maquis, following the trail that wound between the dunes, walking over tufts of dry grass. We ran a few steps and then had to sit down: the sand was burning our feet.

M4. Soon, another blue tent appeared at the top of a bluff, with another boy emerging, sighting us: he waved a red shirt in the air, in the direction of the trees.

M3. In a few minutes, we had reached the maquis. Or rather a little, parched forest; twisted trunks lay fallen, arched, in the sand. We had to bend over double to advance through the thorny branches that cut our backs and sometimes completely blocked the way. Drawn forward and led by the sound of a transistor, we pushed on toward the interior until we reached a clearing.

M4. Sheltered in torn, patched, rudimentary tents, in sleeping bags and even hammocks, no telling how many boys had settled there. Without our even being able to see more than two or three of the inhabitants at once, the grove was seething with people, like a panickly anthill. All along the trails and under the branches, sometimes bent down and lashed together into canopies, youngsters in jersies came and went, hurrying; whenever they passed one another they touched, each pressing an open hand against the other's chest, without a word. They were carrying ropes, stakes, stones, pans and buckets.

M3. They had proclaimed the zone «wild territory».

M4. They weren't armed.

M3. Neither names nor money circulated among them.

M4. Nothing belonged to anyone. They wanted to farm the land. To watch the sunset in silence. Free love.

M3. They feared a repression from the conservative forces that had infiltrated the government.

M4. They had organized their defense in concentric circles. An outer circle, or no-man's land, where enemy movements were tolerated, but closely observed as an alert was sounded. An intermediate circle, where dissuasion was attempted with an accidental rockslide. An inner circle, where they resorted to heavy manoeuvres: sand and fire.

M4. Before withdrawing into the maquis and definitively breaking with the rest of society, they had carried out one final act by rebaptizing the Salazar bridge, at the exit of Lisbon. They smeared macadam over the plaque commemorating the bridge's opening and covered the dictator's name with swastikas.

M3. As the new name, at one end of the bridge, they had adopted: Bakunin. But the more radical element, to render homage to a prophetic novel, had written the name William Burroughs on the opposite pier. Others had proposed Reich, Brecht, and of course Mao, Lenin and Che Guevara.

M4. Once settled in, or withdrawn, behind the dunes, as a security measure, they had maintained one symbolic contact with civilization: the radio, always on.

(In the background, a radio playing Portugese music)

M3. Around the radio, a few, naked and brightly painted, with branches plaited around their heads, mimed a primitive dance, laughing: a feigned ritual. They were shouting, and broke into a round, singing:

M4. Down with the family,
Up with anarchy!

M3. followed by

M4. Freedom! Freedom!

M3. The only time they calmed down was to listen to the news.

(The radio is turned up: three chimes)

M1. *(announcer)* In Angola, the commander-in-chief decided to close a number of military posts located in the uninhabited zones, which offered only a limited interest in the new political situation. The first post abandoned as these measures were executed was Miconje, in the Cabinda district. The communiqué specifies that this action represents a manifestation defined by the President in his speech.

(Three chimes)

M2. Eighteen sailors have lost their lives in the wreck of a Spanish refrigerator ship, the Franco, which sank two days ago, sixty miles north of Villa Cisneros, Spanish Sahara. (Reuter's Wire Service)

(Three chimes)

M1.   A serious motor accident has been reported near Almancil. Six French tourists slipped off the road into a ravine as they rounded a curve at a high speed. This is the second accident of the season in one of the country's most popular vacation areas.

Sound elements
1 - 3 - 5 - 6 - 4 - 2

SEQUENCE IV

W1.   White birds forming a triangle on a background of orange clouds; pupils between the lianas, in the black; iguanas tearing each other apart; scorpions trapped in a circle of fire; and above all — tigers, furious, roaring, bloodthirsty tigers, leaping out from the doubled centerfold at the reader, in hectachrome, with no captions. These were the paper's instructions when they sent us to Africa.

W2.   And what's more, some sequences on the epidemics — a few pustule-eaten heads, cachectic children with swollen bellies, clutching dead birds —, sequences on the drought — skeletal cattle and cracked earth —, sequences on the colonial wars — a querrilla captain posing by stocky blacks with big white teeth, grinning, gleaming with sweat, arms squeezed into red bracelets, machine guns in their fists.

M1.   Quoting Mao, Lenin and Che Guevara in the interviews, of course.

W2.   Searching for rebels, gazelles that flee into the night, pink flamingoes by the thousands, flushed with a rifleshot, on a background just as pink,

M2.   pig-headed ants proliferating,

M1.   and featherless, viscous birds, shoving their beaks up out of splitting eggshells,

M2.   searching for flies with polyhedral eyes, and leeches clinging by the hundreds to a single back,

W1. searching for stomachs shredded by grenades,

M1. corpses covered with white butterflies,

M2. searching for something tacky enough for the magazine section, we had left for Angola; a country, according to the myths of photojournalism, where National Geographic shots for the special September issue would be waiting, as good as pre-centered.

M1. In our jeep, rolling over the savanna at top speed, raising clouds of dust, we «machine-gunned» herds of antelope,

W2. pairs of herons with very long, straight necks,

M1. zebras, in close-up, with color filter:

M2. on an intense, solid blue, acrylic background — hooves, neck, crupper:

M1. parallel bands, blood red, chlorophyll green,

W1. opening around the knee, closing again,

M2. unfolding with the muscles' contraction,

M1. horizontal along the mane,

M2. concentric around the eyes,

M1. blue, deep blue,

W1. cobalt,

W2. on a green and red background of parallel stripes, above the uncertain line of the horizon.

Sound elements
7 - 8

W1. At night, at the end of our strength and curiosity, our bodies clammy, tormented by the heat and the incessant buzzing of insects whose bites we didn't even notice anymore, we took shelter in zinc sheds built along the roadside, where there were folding cots, boiled bushbeans, and cool water that we treated with disinfectant tablets.

M1. As we relaxed after dinner, fragmentary reports reached us, through a nostalgic longing for fans and cold Coca-cola: the last skirmishes in the war for independence. Sometimes Portuguese soldiers went by on the path of retreat, their posts abandoned.

Sound elements
7 - 9 - 8

W1. Excited, a little crazy from thirst and the fermented palm juice, we were following a couple of antelopes at high noon.

W2. The jeep's radio was broadcasting music.

M2. Our cameras were loaded.

M1. We were rolling full speed over the savanna.

W2. Harsh sunlight,

M2. violent colors;

M1. the animals were fleeing, caught between the telescope's coordinates, behind the ciphers, they were crossing the quadrated lense,

M2. gleaming,

M1. like rows of stones, strung together,

M2. spread apart, split:

M1. symmetrical,

M2. silhouettes cut down the middle,

M1. sliced in two.

W1. We were scouring the savanna.

M1. Breathless, drenched,

M2. heads spinning:

M1. the fermented palm juice,

M2. foot on the accelerator,

M1. faster,

M2. nearer,

M1. a more colorful coat,

M2. bigger eyes, dilated,

M1. sharper contours on the blue background,

>*(In the background, a radio playing Portugese music.)*

M1. another filter:

M2. bluer contours,

M1. Zoom:

M2. yellow pupils,

M1. close-up.

>*(A silence)*

W1. And then:

W2. the screeching.

M2. A flip.

M1. A cloud of dust, slow, rising, gyring:

M2. an ochre spiral,

M1. in slow motion.

M2. Silence.

(A silence: the radio is turned up: three chimes)

M3. (*as announcer*) Mister Waldheim will offer Lisbon the services of the United Nations for this event, the most delicate stage of the decolonization process: the transmission of power from the former administrative authorities to the nationalist representatives. Transfer of power to the black majority will be the goal of negotiations between the parties concerned, so that the crowning moment of the decolonization process will be the creation of three nations, whom we hope will live together in the brotherhood of the Portugese language. This was the substance of the declaration delivered on Wednesday by the Portugese Prime Minister, Colonel Gonçalves, during an interview published in the Lisbon evening dailies.

M1. Three flips on the savanna,

M2. spinters of glass on the parched earth,

M1. on tufts of grass the wind blows for kilometers, like spherical nests,

M2. on white feathers,

M1. and gnawed skeletons,

W1. falling splinters of bursting glass,

M1. shining,

M2. on the savanna.

(*A silence*)

W1. Heat,

W2. light,

M1. sharp contours,

M2. sand,

M1. glass,

M2. dust.

Sound elements
7 - 9 - 10 - 8

SEQUENCE V

W2. At night, at the end of our strength and curiosity, our bodies clammy,
tormented by the heat and the incessant buzzing of insects whose bites
we didn't even notice anymore, we took shelter in one of those zinc
sheds built along the roadside, where there were folding cots, boiled
bushbeans, and cool water that treated with disinfectant tablets.

M2. Relaxing after dinner, we listened to two Portugese soldiers, through a
nostalgic longing for fans and cold Coca-cola:

Sound elements
7 - 9 - 11 - 10 - 8

M3. When the Lisbon command ordered us to close the post, there was hardly anything left to take away: a transistor, a primo stove, and three

regulation blankets that had never been much good for anything.

M4. The wicker chairs were caved in, and the zinc shutters were always pulled down.

M3. On the maps that covered the walls, the harsh light and the days' interminable echo had left nothing but the keys and some black letters. In the center of a fan which hadn't moved for years, a wasps' nest. The apparatus gave off a short screech whenever the wind slammed one of the doors, and the same screech was in the window hinges and the drawers of a desk we used for a kitchen cabinet and had stained with grease.

M4. The commander-in-chief had decided to close several military posts that were situated in uninhabited zones, and which were no longer useful in the new political situation.

M3. We received the order to abandon the post while we were having breakfast.

M4. Right away, we started loading the jeeps.

M3. The evacuation didn't surprise us. We were waiting for it.

M4. We had already organized our gradual retreat. In concentric circles.

M3. First, in the course of our daily watches, we had stopped taking any interest at all in an outer circle, which covered several kilometers in all directions; during the past few months, our telescopes had revealed nothing there but a few fleeing animales caught between the coordinates, behind the ciphers, crossing the quadrated lens.

M4. And then we stopped going out to the intermediate circle: the area around the post. We cut the nocturnal rounds to a minimum, and a single soldier kept watch during the day.

M3. The inner circle coincided with the *territory* marked of by the urine of Absurdo, a white dog who had been with us for the last few years. White and mute.

M4. This last trait, a little unusual for a military post's watchdog, earned him his name.

M3. Absurdo appeared one night, dusty and thirsty, scratching at the gate. He had yellow eyes, as dry as glass marbles. He was wagging his tail.

M4. We never found out where he came from. The nearest hamlet was several dozen kilometers away; its inhabitants, who would have feasted on birds' eggs, and who depended on the rain and the parched, blistered earth, couldn't raise anything but starving cattle with wrinkled hides draped across their jutting ribs.

M3. As usual, Absurdo had breakfast with us.

M4. He drank.

M3. As always at that hour — he stayed awake all night long —, he came out into the courtyard to sleep.

M4. We waited until he was sound asleep,

M3. until his breathing slowed down, and his body abandoned itself to its full weight on the ground.

M4. We approached carefully,

M3. on tip-toe,

M4. step by step, without breathing, almost: we knew how acute his hearing was.

(*A silence*)

M3. We fired.

(*A silence*)

M4. We buried him next to a tree where he used to bury bones he would save for weeks, and then gnaw once they were rotten.

M3. We threw an open can of sardines and a packet of sugar into the trench, along with his green plastic plate.

M4. We piled the dirt back up. It wasn't very late in the morning yet.

M3. And then, so we could lower it again, we raised the faded flag that testified to our years of presence there,

M4. a greenish rag,

M3. old and pink,

M4. that once was blood red,

M3. chlorophyll green.

M4. On a background of blue-grey clouds, with no birds,

M3. slowly, the rectangle unfolded, slowly,

M4. in slow motion,

M3. frayed at the edges,

M4. washed out by the wind.

M3. And then, it came back down within reach of our hands.

M4. We rolled it up.

M3. We packed it into the back of the jeep.

M4. Toward noon, we started the jeeps.

M3. We watched the post fade in the distance,

M4. the parched trees all around it,

M3. the hill it sat on top of.

M4. We wanted to celebrate the closing of the post.

M3. All we could find to drink was a few bottles of fermented palm juice, in a zinc shed by the roadside. We left again right away.

M4. We got back into the jeeps.

M3. At high noon.

M4. We headed off into the savanna,

M3. breathless, drenched,

M4. heads spinning.

M3. The fermented palm juice.

M4. We caught sight of fleeing animals, in the distance.

M3. The wind blew up tufts of dried grass.

M4. We turned on the radio: the news from Lisbon.

M3. We were pushing the motor. In the rear-view mirror, we could see hills go by, the unchanging ochre of the earth, the dead straight lines traced by our wheels.

M4. A cloud of dust.

Sound elements
7 - 9 - 11 - 12 - 10 - 8

SEQUENCE VI

W1. It was a spectacular accident, but harmless in the end. The radio exaggerated a lot, no doubt to frighten the reckless into being more careful. True, the sight could not fail to make a certain impression; nor, for the esthetically inclined, to recall the compressed cars of Cesar. The car had flipped over at the top of a curve overlooking Almancil, and lay there, crushed.

W2. Colored glass covered the roadway, like raindrops after a storm. The searchlights were tracing two yellow parallels across the ground. The local crockery we had just bought had scattered colonial landscapes across the macadam. The horn and radio were jammed, emitting a continuous, shrill whistle, already wavering, like a toy train's, and spouting local news, with Spanish interference and flurries of static.

M1. Two soldiers in a jeep picked us up. They gave us a bittersweet, urine-colored fermented juice to drink, to help us put ourselves back together — they said they'd brought it back from Africa.

M2. The next day, bruised and bandaged, in a rented car, we were back on the road to Lisbon.

M3. Portugal doesn't offer many resources these days, for the hasty visitor, eager to bring back slides with at least a touch of red. Nothing, of the ongoing transformation, affects the reality seized by a camera. No banners marked with flowered rifles, no monumental inscriptions, no daily parades.

M4. And yet men crowd into the cafes, in their shirtsleeves, around the radio.

W1. We had to settle for shots of Manueline façades: ropes and seashells, armillary spheres, Indian birds.

W2. As we were entering Lisbon, we stopped on the Salazar bridge:

M1. the inevitable zoom on the Belem tower.

W2. We were about to start up again, when in front of the car, right at the end of the bridge, a bare-chested boy rose up.

M1. Barefoot, big teeth; long hair, ruffled, blond, burnt.

M2. Covered with bracelets and African chokers.

M1. Staring at us, threatening, slow, he raised his hands, and carefully, as if in slow motion, unfolded a red fabric with green fringes: a shirt, perhaps.

W1. We turned around. At the other end of the bridge, despite the distance, the same signal clearly answered him.

M1. The bridge had been closed.

M2. Without realizing it, we had penetrated a forbidden circle.

M3. Behind the standard-bearer, other boys rose up, half-naked, face and feet painted black, with strange hats made of branches.

W1. They were singing, but we didn't understand the words.

W2. Nor why they signaled us to stop: they weren't asking for money, and had no leaflets to hand out.

M1. Nor did we understand why, a little later, the boy folded the shirt back up and signaled us to go on.

M2. I was driving. We were advancing slowly. I had turned on the radio. I was waiting for it to give us an explanation. He was holding his red shirt rolled up in his right hand, like a rag. He slipped his left hand in the window, and struck me on the chest, as if to print an emblem on my sweater. That was all.

M3. They were all singing. They were carrying a bucket of macadam, and on their backs, bundles of bedrolls and provisions.

M4. They were advancing in single file. All in step. Like blindmen.

M1. They passed by the car without even glancing at us.

W1. In the rear-view mirror we watched them fade in the distance:

M1. identical,

M2. in rows,

M3. eager, and hurrying.

M1. Several were carrying a heavy bundle, straining, wavering, leaning against each other,

M2. and sometimes giving way;

M3. others, hurrying, came to replace those who fell.

M4. The bundle advanced.

M1. without touching the ground,

M2. on outstretched arms, like a trophy,

M3. like an insect's corpse,

M4. or a lump of sugar.

Sound elements
7 - 9 - 11 - 12 - 10 - 8